the time he was a child in his native African village, through his education, transition to the corporate world, introduction to Jesus and the Christian faith, and finally his marriage to a beautiful Christian woman. Imma's story reflects what most of us face in life - challenges, hurts, traumas, disappointments, and successes. It is a great reminder that life is a journey complete with trials and successes and requires sincere faith in God to truly find deep meaning and ultimate satisfaction!

David Taylor, P.Eng.
Founder, Thinking Business Calgary & Author, Strength Zone

Great book! Very well written. The story of Imma is an honest look at the struggle on the journey to faith that many of us have faced, or know someone who has, or is going through that journey. It is both encouraging and enlightening and I would highly recommend others to read this story. It will give others an insight into the struggle to find true freedom. This freedom is free, but it's not easy. Imma's journey proves that and he is not alone.

Kelly Stickel,
Author & Senior Pastor, My Victory Lethbridge, Alberta Canada

Path to the Dream Life

ANAYO ONWUKA

ENDORSEMENTS

This is a well written book by Pastor Anayo. It is a refreshing true to life story of many who wish to live the Dream. This book is intriguing. From the very beginning it draws you in so that you want to know more. What happens next, you find yourself wondering. A good read indeed!

Dr. Hazel Lurline Deborah Hill, Director VCI Missions & Author
vcimissions@victoryusa.org, www.victorychildrenshomes.com,
www.victoryint.tv

Anayo Onwuka introduces Imma, an ambitious young African on a quest to find personal and familial respect, professional success and spiritual fulfillment. Mr. Onwuka's incisive writing takes readers through Imma's trials and tribulations in such a compelling and engaging manner that it's difficult not to root for his likable protagonist as he searches for his place in the world. With keen insight, impressive pacing and a dash of humor Mr. Onwuka presents a narrative that resonates.

Uche Uwah
TV News Producer, WRC-TV, Washington DC

Anayo Onwuka spins an intriguing story in the lingo of his native Africa. The story unfolds around the faith journey of Imma from

I thoroughly enjoyed this book. The story is fast-moving and the way you described the different characters is vivid and I could just picture them as I read. I also enjoyed the humorous voice you gave to the lead character and his friends - had me laughing out loud several times as I read.

Uzoma Uponi
Author, ColourBlind & Whispers from Yesteryears

O the depth of the riches both of the wisdom and knowledge of God! How unsearchable are His judgements, and His ways are past finding out!' Romans 11:33. Indeed the steps of the righteous are ordered of God. The simplicity, beautiful imagery, relatable events, and vibrant language make this book such a delight to read! Paths to the Dream Life is a must read for every believer or would-be believer. A book you hate to put down....

Vera Edobor
Educationist & Author, The Best Day Ever!

Anayo has told a lovely, easy to read story of a young Nigerian village boy, Imma faced with the "normal" African challenge: poverty. As I read through, I had deep personal reflections and on the Bible story of Jacob who was forced to flee home to an unknown place. While on his way, an encounter with the Lord totally changed the course of his life story. This book is a simple story that should provoke deep thoughts (or perhaps a controversy) on the place and role of faith in achieving our life goals.

Chidi Fabian Aleke,
Pastor, He's Alive Chapel Lagos Nigeria & Budding Author

Almost every successful man or woman of our generation (especially from economically emerging nations like Nigeria) must have passed through the ferocious fires of economic deprivation, social cold wars of self-identification, religious pressures of faith navigation, and the ethical/moral wars of balancing between right/wrong and economic emancipation. The story of Imam as presented in this book by Pastor Oliver Onwuka is typical of many who would be privileged to read it. In this book, Imam is a living testimony to the popular saying by Norman Vincent Pearle that: "Empty pockets never held anyone back, only empty heads and empty hearts can do that". The story confirms that the world clears and makes a way for those who know where they are going and that a small but consistent step in the right direction is a sure way to reach one's destination, of course with God's Grace as the guiding light. This book is a rare blend of humor, grammar and discourse on serious contemporary issues. I recommend this piece to all, especially our youths, as a proof that what the mind can conceive, it can achieve.

Chidi Osuji, Pharmacist & Author,
A Unique and Simplified Approach to Pharmacy Calculations for
Healthcare Professionals

Path to the Dream Life will educate and entertain you. As the author explores Imma's journey towards a closer relationship with Jesus Christ, the reader, like Imma, learns many valuable lessons, including perhaps the most valuable lesson of all…to find life, you must first lose your life. I highly recommend this book to Believers as well as Non-Believers alike!

Chinwe Williams Ph.D., LPC, NCC, CPCS, EMDR trained
Counselor Educator & Supervisor, Cumming GA USA

"Path to the Dream Life" is fresh, inviting, captivating and thought provoking. It challenges the reader to assess the meaning of success in one's life. What does it mean to be successful - material accumulation at all cost or faithful achievements, through peace, joy and contentment? I recommend this book to anyone and everyone, especially to young people on the quest to chart their own life paths.

Moji Taiwo, Author
I Give Because I'm Blessed, I'm Blessed Because I Give: A
Chronicle of An Immigrant's Journey

*Path to the Dream Life made a very enjoyable reading. This is a
good work with a story line that will minister to readers on the
issue of transiting from mere Churchgoers to truly saved people.*

Dr. EmmaJoe Nwachukwu,
Director, Missions Aid International & Writer

Paperback ISBN: 978-1-9995199-1-9
eBook ISBN: 978-1-9995199-0-2

Publisher

Immanuel (IISI) Publishing
A Division of Immanuel Integrated Services Inc.
Calgary, Alberta Canada
info@iintservices.com
www.iintservices.com

DEDICATION

To
my dad, Hyacinth Chilaka Onwuka – teacher and writer,
& my cousin, Aloysius Chukwuma Okoro - lecturer and John F. Kennedy
Essay contest winner:
You both are not here, but are still here…your passion for words still
inspires me!

And to
my Treasures - Wife, Chinyere; Son, Chinonyeranyi & Daughter, Favour:
You are my Dream Team!

Contents

ACKNOWLEDGMENTS

Writing coaches advise to avoid clichés like, it takes a village, in order to not starve creativity. The only creative thing I can come up with right now is, it takes the globe.

Indeed, it took more than a village to write this book! You are too m many to fit into this acknowledgement page, hence would graciously, agree, wouldn't you, to be represented by the few mentioned?

Brandy Petch, BP (met her in BP Canada) fired, 'sign me up for a copy and make sure you autograph it'. Maja Bruggencate, my Leader at TransCanada, asked, 'are you publishing the book? Cool; fingers crossed'. Colleagues, business associates and friends like Olga Krzhipova, Mark Jergeas, Wairimu Kihuyu, Noel de Jesus, Sam Jans, Anthony Ramos, Woinshet Habtemariam, Sheila Addiscot. Deba Eigbe, Kevin Hendershot, Les Bischoff, Todd Anderson, Lucia Mena, Mavis Egege, Chuks Ejiogu, KC Uwazie, Smartress Chikwendu, Nkem Ejiofor, Chika Onwuekwe, Austin Omobhude: checked in, encouraged, cajoled. Wendell Klassen, TransCanada Director wrote, 'I look forward to enjoying it'. Pressure. How could I not complete this book?

These, you invested your precious time to critique this book and provided valuable feedback, for which my Professional Editor, Rod Chapman (https://rodchapman.com/) and I are very grateful:

Annie Oortman (www.annieedits.com), who assured, 'Editing is a bitch. I'm not.' Jim Watkins www.jameswatkins.com (after your feedback, I was downcast for two weeks but glad for how it led to this rewrite) Emeka Casimir Onwuka (Martin Luther King Jr's. I have a Dream enriched this book because of you). Tatenda Mawoyo. Tyler Pawsey. Jeremy Cheyne. Amaka Thomas. Nneka Onwu. Wayne King Pele Williams. Kelly Stickel. Toyin Odufeso. Chidinma Imegwu. Anele Ebizie. Ivanna Ihekwoaba. Hadiza Amedu-Ode. Chinwe Williams. Uche Uwah. Manie Azenda. James Arukhe. Somi Gbadamosi. Paul MacDonald. Cristayne Tsuu, EmmaJoe Nwachukwu. Emma Onuoha. Chidi Aleke. Sylvia Mawoyo. Seun

Ajibode. Uzoma Uponi. Vera Edobor. Cindy Wagner, Randy Vandervoort …

Many thanks to the numerous Beta (test) Readers, Book Title survey participants and cover design image assessors!

I appreciate Kikelola Emechafor, who developed the cover design that helped the professional cover designer's work. Stephen Ajibowu, the Author picture photographer.

My gratitude to my friends - Hilary Azoba who was sure I had a thing for writing, and Chima who insisted on an end date to this project, suspecting I was coasting. He never heard of writer's block!

My sisters Nkechi, Chinedu, Uzoma, Chika and Onyinye cheered, prophesied over and encouraged me, and my immediate older brother Chidi pushed me…just get it published!

For all that prayed for me, including my Kingdom Life Victory Church family: blessings!

And to my Dream Team: Chiny, Chino, Favour & Abby, what can I say? We did it! Luv y'all lots!

1

How it all Began

The day began like any other for Imma Chibundu Vine. Three months already since the impossible had happened. Today he was eager to connect with a bright, rich acquaintance. Imma had learned to respect the advantages of being close to the strong and wealthy. Twice already, he had been rescued by his connections to such people after having his ambition blow up in his face.

Dressed in his unmistakable expensive black shoes, black trouser and blue shirt, IkeChi Ndu was already seated in the Nnamdi Azikiwe hostel buttery when Imma arrived. Settling down to their order of fried fish, plantain chips and soft drinks, IkeChi leaned forward and pointed to Imma's head.

"Are those white hair I see?"

"May be," Imma said, laughing.

"You're not old. Too much studying?"

Imma stroked his hair.

"I wish. But I've had these wisdom hair forever – birth mark."

Imma, seventeen years old, five feet eight, light-skinned and on the thin side, had full black hair except for that patch on the left side.

IkeChi took a gulp of his *Just Juice.*

"Tell me about your family."

That's blunt, Imma thought. From the few times they had met, he should have seen it coming. Hesitating, Imma said, "No, you go first."

"I'm from Ogbunike, near Ogidi, Anambra State. Family of three and my parents graduated from this university..."

"Is that why you chose here?"

"You could say so. I can see my two siblings coming here as well."

"First time away from home?"

"Yes. My parents are nervous. They've visited every other weekend, and I'm beginning to feel embarrassed."

"Why? I dream of getting my family to visit me here."

"Everybody has started calling me Daddy's and Mommy's boy. It isn't funny! Can't wait till I get the car they promised so I can zoom home to see them instead."

Imma's ears perked and he peered into IkeChi. "A car? Your family must dote on you! Mine loves me too but they won't be buying me a car – ever."

IkeChi laughed.

"Too many people and too little money? How many?"

Imma chuckled. "Where I come from, the correct answer is, 'we don't count children'."

"Clever! Come on, tell me."

"Bad things can happen if I break my people's rule."

"You don't look the superstitious type."

"Okay. Nine."

IkeChi's mouth snapped open and his eyes widened.

"Those must be nine deprived children!"

Imma hushed.

At first they laughed about it, but as they rode home on IkeChi's motorcycle Imma defended his parents and the dignity of his family. Stopping at IkeChi's room, they watched television and played pop songs from an out-of-this-world – well, out-of-Imma's-world – music system. Helping themselves from IkeChi's lavishly stocked refrigerator, envy and inspiration surged through Imma. He took it all in – the album filled with colourful photos of family vacations overseas. Beautiful wallpaper. Richly stocked wardrobe. The reading table containing all the recommended books for his courses, and more.

On the way to his hostel, Imma couldn't shake the word *deprived* echoing in his head. His bare-bones room and reading table contained the one solitary textbook he had been able to buy so far. He fell onto the bed and buried his face in the pillow, allowing sleep to wash over him. Waking up early the next day, tears swept away his desire to be connected to IkeChi. In solemn defiance, Imma penned an entry in his red diary:

December 5, 1979. University of Nigeria, Nsukka.

No one will ever again describe me or my family as deprived.
Never again.

Going to the lecture hall, Iwunze, Imma's project team member on a GS 101 - General Studies English Language course – confronted him.

"You didn't show up for our assignment last night."

"Forgive me, I forgot. Met a friend in the evening, then went straight to bed."

Iwunze drew close and whispered.

"She wore you out?"

Imma pushed him away.

"Worse. He wounded my soul."

"He? Who? How?"

"I don't want to talk about it."

"That's your business. My concern is that we're behind on this project because you didn't show up. Be ready to take the blame if we fail to get an A in this course."

"I apologize – we won't! I will make it up to the group. Can't miss this opportunity for an A."

In the nineteen-year history of the university's Department of Economics, no one had achieved a first-class degree. Every new class dreamed of breaking the jinx. Imma and his team had made it their goal: at their graduation ceremony in four years, at least one of them would be awarded a first-class degree. More than ever, Imma wanted that person to be him. IkeChi had something to do with that.

From that December 5 to the end of his three-month first term on December 21, Imma grinded away and hustled. When he learnt of another student, Frank, who created a side business bringing in shoes and clothing to sell on campus, Imma was inspired. *Light bulb.* Unable to buy his own merchandise as a re-seller, he joined the bustle as a sales generator, earning minimum commission on his contacts' purchases from Frank. Other than that and one campus Christmas party, Imma just attended lectures, studied and slept some - a cycle that would mark the rest of his undergraduate life.

Before the end of that first term as well, someone from Imma's family visited him! His roommate had responded to a gentle knock on the door.

"*Sister*!" Imma shouted, almost knocking her down with a big hug. Chidubem was Imma's second sister.

"Imma, good to see you. How have you been?"

"Great, but have been missing home. So glad you came. I wondered if anyone would visit…"

"I've been planning this visit for a while. Mama and Papa wanted me to come, but it had to wait. Arrears of teachers' salaries were paid just this week."

"Thank you so much. I see that your bag is fat. Lots of things for me?"

"Open it. I'm sure you'll share with your roommates and friends."

In Chidubem's bag was an array of home-made food, fresh fruits, and snacks.

"Wow, this is my best day in university yet!"

"The fresh food and fruits are from our farm."

Imma grimaced. "Many thanks, *Sister*, but let's not talk about farming."

One person and just once, but a family visit nonetheless. And timing was great, as Imma had wondered if he would have enough money to transport himself home for Christmas. Chidubem made sure of that. Even better, Christmas could not have come earlier for him: he has now crossed off family visit on the mental list of advantages IkeChi held over him.

Over the following terms, Imma received more visitors – among them his childhood friends Umunna, Chukwuemeka, LuChi and Nath. It meant a lot to Imma that his friends would make the effort to come see him, some travelling many hours at great expense.

And, there was that other visitor in the last term of his program. Propitious.

Godson Nwaka was a Professor of Mathematics and Dean of Graduate Studies at the University of Jos, six hours away from the University of Nigeria's Nsukka campus. Among Imma's few privileges in life was that the only professor then in his village was also his godfather. Prof took his *mentoring* duties seriously, doting on Imma and even visiting him in secondary school.
Still, when his roommate shook him awake, Imma almost jumped out of his skin.

"Prof!"

"Young man, it's just 9:30 pm."

"I do most of my studying in the day and early mornings. My alarm is set for 4 am." Imma rubbed his eyes as he pulled up a chair for Prof.

"I believe you. You know what it took for you to be here."

Imma eased himself to the edge of his bed and dropped his head.

"Yes, Prof. Don't make me relive that…"

"I won't. Just don't let us – or yourself - down."

Prof had come for a conference, but he had managed to stop by to bestow another privilege on his protégé. Imma was certain IkeChi hadn't received a visitor of that calibre.

One more up on IkeChi.

The four-year undergraduate degree program completed, Auntie Joanne, Imma's closest wealthy connection and benefactor did him another great favour. She sent her car to take him home – in style.

On the narrow dirt road passing through farms with chirping birds announcing his arrival, Imma retreated into the mental journey of his university sojourn. The admission that he took up by the skin of his teeth; the outside help, the family sacrifice, the vacation jobs that paid for it all. Barely. Recalling being called a 'triangular' student, he smiled. Tethering himself to a routine of studying, eating and sleeping, he had given his all in pursuit of a first-class degree. In his tropical African country of Nigeria, that degree was a passport to immediate employment in the university or in the corporate world. A passport to a dream life!

Auntie Joanne's driver sounded the horn, announcing his arrival. A crowd gathered to welcome Imma and celebrate with his family. In this part of the world, and in that era, university education was still a major accomplishment, a success owned by the whole village.

Imma knew it was only a matter of time before the conversation happened. At dinner, his dad said, "Welcome home again, son. We are so glad you have graduated."

"I am too, Papa. It has not been easy. I am thankful for the sacrifice and support from so many."

"How was your result?"

Imma took another scoop of food, filled his mouth, and chewed.

"Do you want to finish eating before you chat?"

"Oh, my result? I got a second class upper; missed first class by fractions."

"Did anybody make a first class?"

"Yes, one classmate, Chuma Azoba. Well deserved – he's really smart and worked very hard."

"Oh."

Papa sat quietly with lowered eyes. An elementary school teacher, he was known for lots of words, emotion and even drama. But now, he gave away nothing. Not even the jaw tightening that Imma could see from a distance the few times his dad was upset. After what seemed like an eternity, he picked up Imma's suitcase and left the room without looking at his son. Imma wasn't fooled. Papa's sadness and disappointment in his academic performance was palpable.

Imma's grade-point average – second-best in his graduating class – wasn't bad, but that was cold comfort. Now Imma needed to set his sights on the next challenge: seeking job opportunities to pave the way for the life he craved.

That was until a conversation with Professor Godson. His godfather had been promoted again, and was now vice chancellor at a federal university in the northeastern region of the country.

"Congratulations, young man. We all expected that you would make a first class, though."

"I know. I'm disappointed too, but…"

"Don't worry about it. Your result looks good enough to get you admission for graduate studies in a good university."

"I'm not even thinking of graduate studies. Who will pay for that? All I want is to get a good job, start helping my family and, frankly, provide a good life for myself for a change."

"You don't have to worry about who will pay if you get a scholarship. With good GMAT or GRE scores and a strong recommendation, you should get a scholarship."

"GMAT, GRE…what are those?"

"Graduate Management Admissions Test and Graduate Records Examination. They are aptitude tests required for graduate school admission in the United States."

"United States?"

"Yes, my friends and colleagues are in several universities there. If you do your part, I can provide a strong recommendation to get you scholarships that will cover your tuition and living expenses. And I have no doubt that you'll work hard to do well and get a good job there to take care of yourself and help your family."

"School and work in the United States?"

"Yes. Like I did."

Imma almost fell off his chair.

Lying that night on a *king* bed in the luxury guest room at the *Vice Chancellor's Lodge* after a sumptuous chef-prepared and served meal, Imma recalled Prof's visit to him in university.

He had said, '…don't let us or yourself down.' *Was he hinting at America? Auspicious!*

In his sleep, the American dream took a hold of Imma.

In the one week he spent with them, Prof and family were very kind to Imma. Staying up close with them and their four kids, Imma for the first time got a feel of people that had schooled and lived in America. His wife, respectfully called 'Madam' by most, was persistent in getting to eat lots.

"You need to fill out your flesh a little bit. Otherwise they may not allow you into America."

"She's joking," Prof said, putting Imma at ease.

Madam agreed, but added, "I notice that you didn't respond timely to invite for meals and ended up eating after us. We like to eat together. Don't be a stranger."

"Pardon me; I'll make sure to join at the next meal."

Prof put a hand on the shoulder of his godson. "Feel at home, young man."

What they didn't know was how intimidating their large dining table was. The very rich menus sometimes included pancake, pasta, sandwich, coleslaw, Caesar salad topped with a *thousand island* dressing, yoghurt and ice cream – many totally new to Imma. He relished the aroma and sight of them, but was embarrassed that he didn't know how they were eaten. Nor whether he would like them, or they him – by remaining in his stomach! When he ate alone, he went for the familiar. However, determined to not offend in any way these kind, highly placed people key to the fulfilment of his dreams, Imma decided to get bold ask questions and learn. *My acclimatization for America has begun.*

In the many months that followed, Imma began applying to American universities. His compulsory post-university National Youth Service gave him time to study for GRE. Then Iowa State University offered him admission and a scholarship to cover his first year tuition!

Four days to the visa interview, Imma travelled to his Umuoma village home from his national service post at Uyo, Akwa Ibom State. He picked up some key documents for the trip and enjoyed a welcome break to the twelve hour Bus ride to the US Consulate location, Lagos - Nigeria's largest city of ten million people. Wide awake late into the night before his departure, he got a panorama of his room under the light of the kerosene lamp. Training his sight on a framed photo of his university graduation on the wall, a crease formed on his face as he smiled in self-appreciation. *Not bad.*

The journey the next morning traversed six states in three regions of the country – Imo and Anambra in the South East, Delta and Edo in the South South, and Ondo and Ogun in the South West -- to get to Lagos, also in the South West. *For this long dream, no problem covering this much real estate,* Imma mused.

Sleeping and snacking in *The Young Shall Grow* luxury bus, Imma nodded and imagined life in America and beyond. *'Am growing indeed. But long ways to go still. Imma, long ways…*

A tropical warm weather pattern had hit the city of Lagos, but Imma found himself breaking out in cold sweat. Today was the day for his US student visa interview. *Just get this visa, and in a few weeks I will be in America!* Today he would put himself and his family on the path to prosperity.

Imma arrived early at the US consulate. He had never been to a big city and was not prepared for the sea of human beings in Lagos. Nor for the queue at the consulate that snaked around the block, everybody trying to go to America.

Three hours later, Imma presented himself to the visa officer.

"Why do you want to go to the United States?"

Didn't he read my visa application?

"To pursue graduate studies at Iowa State University."

"I see. You have admission already. Have you remitted all the funds to cover your program?"

"I got a scholarship and the documents are attached to the application."

"I see that, but the scholarship will cover your tuition for one year only. Do you have evidence of funds that will cover your other expenses?"

"No sir. I expect to find part-time work."

"There's no guarantee that will happen. I'm afraid I can't give you a visa."

Before Imma could open his mouth to plead his case, the stamp came down hard on his passport. The sound was the worst he had heard in twenty-two years of life. Worse even than the rooster crows announcing the ungodly time to go to the farm.

Not going to America.

Leaving the consulate, Imma found a bus stop at the end of the street. Thirty minutes later he got on a bus. A man who sat next to him tried to make conversation but gave up when Imma closed his eyes. He wished sleep would come, but his racing mind denied him that respite.

An announcement by the driver jolted Imma. He fished out the paper on which his oldest brother's friend had written the routes. *Wrong bus!* He scampered out, but it was several hours before he found the right one, getting to his host's home late in the evening.

His host sighed. "Young man, what took you so long? I wondered if you had decided to head to America straight from there."

Imma threw everything he was clutching on the table, and sank into the nearest chair. "Long story…"

"Give me the short version."

"I didn't get the visa, and I got on the wrong bus."

"What? Why?"

As Imma bit into the food his host insisted on, he shared it all. "That's the kind of day it has been. Very disappointed, for sure."

"Not to worry. Contact your godfather and the university. Perhaps they can give you additional documents that will enable you re-apply and convince the consulate."

Sleep eluded Imma. History was repeating itself. Secondary school entry: struggle. Undergraduate university entry: near-miss. Now, graduate school: entry denied.

Am I jinxed?

As his weary soul and body succumbed to sleep, Imma murmured a prayer that providence would show up again for him. It had better, because, certain of going to America immediately upon completion of the one-year compulsory National Youth Service, he had waved off all job opportunities in Nigeria. In two months, the youth service would end.

If I don't get this visa where do I go? Not to the village!

The next day he made the decision to make another long trip to Yola, Adamawa State, to see Professor Godson.

All the way to his godfather's home the next weekend, Imma prayed for a miracle. For good luck. Whatever it was that had salvaged his secondary school and undergraduate university attendance opportunities. *Please do it again!*

And the cross-country luxury bus he rode this time had the logo and name of the transport company emblazoned all over it. *Osondu,* a word in Imma's Igbo language that means, *race of life.*

Such a metaphor. For this trip. For Imma's dream. And life.

"Welcome again, young man. All ready to move to America?"

"Not yet, Prof"

"Why not?"

Professor Godson listened keenly as Imma recounted his ordeal at the US consulate. But before Imma made his appeal, Prof slammed him with the heartbreaking reality.

"Sorry, young man, I have exhausted all my contacts. If you don't have the personal or family funds required by the consulate, I'm afraid you may have to focus on getting a job in Nigeria. Don't beat yourself up – it's not the end of the world. We tried."

When the conversation with his godfather ended, Imma amused himself trying to determine which day was the worst of his life. The day at age twelve when his parents wanted to send him to learn a trade? The day at age seventeen when undergraduate university admission results were announced and he didn't even bother to check? The day at age eighteen when Ike labelled him a deprived child? Or today, at twenty-two, when Prof uttered the words that put paid to his dream of going to America?

Nail in the coffin?

The day after, tail between legs, Imma caught the next available bus back home. In the two months finishing up the National Youth Service, neither fate nor providence showed up. Reconciling himself to pursuing the dream life in Nigeria, he dispatched more than fifty job applications, but did not receive a single response.

Then a light bulb came on. In secondary school, a few alumni returned as auxiliary teachers. Crowning his secondary school academic record with posting the school's best result in the final year had endeared him to the principal and teachers. Calculating his chances, Imma was convinced that if there was a vacancy for a temporary teacher, he would be a number-one candidate. That would not be a dream job or life, but he would be in Makurdi, far from his village and from the farm.

2

A Dream Deferred

One month later Imma was on his way to take up the position of auxiliary teacher in his alma mater, Mount Saint Gabriel's Secondary School, in Makurdi. Settling in for the long trip, he was bemused at the irony staring him in the face. Becoming a student here ten years ago was like being raised from the dead. And now he was going to be a teacher. Memories of Imma's miracle – rescue number one – came flooding back.

Lifting up teary eyes to the heavens as the taxi dropped him off at the staff quarters of the school, Imma thanked providence. As a student, Imma studied hard. He shunned parties, movies, and all the teenage years' troubles, finishing best in the school and winning several awards. He was glad that the awards justified the confidence cousin Mark placed in him. But today he was happy that they had earned him a job – and an escape from the village and the farm.

The ragged, red diary followed Imma to Makurdi, tucked away among his most prized possessions. Regularly he fished it out and re-read that December 5, 1979 entry. *Never again.*

Imma's seventeen-month auxiliary teaching stint in Makurdi was packed with regular classes in the school and part-time evening and weekend tutorial jobs. The deprived label, and his vow, were front and centre in his mind. Two months in, he brought a younger sister to complete her education with his sponsorship. Déjà vu. And he regularly sent his widow's mite home to support the family financially. Payback time. *Deprivation relief.*

One year after his godfather had planted that possibility in his heart, the going-to-America dream still had a grip on Imma. Jostling and hustling in Makurdi, he earned enough to afford multiple applications to American universities, re-register for GRE and register for GMAT. He threw wide the net for admission, larger scholarships, graduate assistantships and hence a visa. Shunning almost all social life, the city library became Imma's second home.

The library rewarded Imma's patronage. Newspapers didn't fit into his budget but two chance readings of some in the library presented him with two opportunities to further pull himself up. In a United States Information Service advertisement for a Martin Luther King Jr. birthday essay contest, Imma saw a visa application booster. In a bank posting for management trainees, he saw a higher earning and savings opportunity. Vowing to let neither opportunity slip through his fingers, Imma logged more hours at the library.

One month later he made the eight-hour trip from Makurdi to Benin to write the bank job selection aptitude test. Finding himself in the midst of a sea of candidates for the advertised twenty positions, he broke into cold sweat. But that turned into a big smile as the questions began to look familiar. The countless hours on those GRE and GMAT practice questions were going to pay off even bigger!

What followed was a roller-coaster of events that nearly derailed this dream. The bank's workers' union protested against the recruitment of external candidates, and a lobby group demanded the exclusion of non-indigene employees. Nevertheless, twelve months after submitting his application, Imma thanked the Human Resources lady and collected his bank access card.

"Congratulations. You are a very smart and lucky young man."

"Thanks so much."

"From more than 2,000 applicants we employed only ten instead of the twenty candidates we had planned to hire – and just two of those ten were non-indigenes of the state."

Thanking her again, Imma made his exit. A few metres away from the building he found a place to sit down and reflect. He was a non-indigene. What odds had he just surmounted? He fished the bank access card out of his bag and took a closer look at his photo with the words, "Staff, New Nigeria Bank, Benin." Leaning over a fence he looked up to the sky, teary-eyed.

A colleague shouted over the office cubicle. "Imma, have you seen today's papers?"

"No. Why?"

"Hurry over!"

Imma was quick to catch the newspaper.

"Take a look at the front page – you're the happening guy, my man!"

Staring at Imma was a photo of himself and the director of the United States Information Service.

"Oh, wow. Front page. Never could have imagined…."

"First prize. And a journalist was second. What are you doing here in a bank?"

"Chasing the dream like everybody else."

"Congrats, man! Your village must be very proud!"

"For sure," Imma choked.

Borrowing the newspaper from his colleague, Imma went over to his manager, Mr. Matt Ifeanyichukwu.

"Have you seen this yet, sir?"

"What?"

"The papers carried reports of the essay prize award ceremony. Here."

The manager jumped up and gripped Imma in a firm handshake. "My goodness, this is great! Congratulations, young man!"

"Thank you sir; and thanks again for allowing me time to travel to Lagos for the ceremony. Means a lot to me."

"Not just to you, but to the bank as well. I know you wrote this essay before you joined the bank. However, the award ceremony and newspaper reports happened after you got here. This will be good publicity for the bank. Hold on!"

A phone call and a few minutes later Imma found himself before the bank's Assistant General Manager, Administration. He had never seen an office of that grandeur. Responding to a request to use the award photo for the bank's corporate promotion campaign, Imma blurted out, "I'd be honoured, sir."

A week after his meeting with the bank's management, the local television station carried the award photo and story. During the evening news Imma sat open-mouthed, glued to the television. He was in a photo on TV with an American diplomat. This was not in his ragged, red journal. This was not in the script.

A few of the monetary allowances Imma was entitled to in the bank, not counting his base salary, exceeded all his primary and hustling earnings in his teaching job. He started saving up for supplemental funding toward going to America. The prestige, higher earnings, and job advancement potential did nothing to break the hold of the going-to-America dream on him.

In the celebration of the essay contest win, Imma was careful to hide his disappointment in the prize. In the library when he first saw the essay contest advertisement, he had harboured a hope that the prize would advance his bigger dream – but the hundred US dollars and Martin Luther King 'I have a Dream' poster and book fell short. A scholarship, or a visit to Martin Luther King's city of Atlanta, would have gone a long way toward furthering Imma's own American dream. He rued his hard luck.

With his longstanding interest in the American icon and the many essay preparation hours poring over his 'I have a Dream' speech of August 28, 1963 at the *March on Washington for Jobs and Freedom*, Imma knew some parts of it by heart. Seeking some inspiration to uplift him from the looming despondency, he recited them.

....I say to you today, my friends, so even though we face the difficulties of today and tomorrow, I still have a dream. It is a dream deeply rooted in the American dream.

I have a dream that one day this nation will rise up and live out the true meaning of its creed: "We hold these truths to be self-evident; that all men are created equal."

I have a dream that one day on the red hills of Georgia the sons of former slaves and the sons of former slave owners will be able to sit down together at the table of brotherhood.

I have a dream that one day even the state of Mississippi, a state sweltering with the heat of injustice, sweltering with the heat of oppression, will be transformed into an oasis of freedom and justice.

I have a dream that my four little children will one day live in a nation where they will not be judged by the color of their skin but by the content of their character.

I have a dream today.

I have a dream that one day down in Alabama, with its vicious racists, with its governor having his lips dripping with the words of interposition and nullification, that one day right down in Alabama little black boys and black girls will be able to join hands with little white boys and white girls as sisters and brothers.

I have a dream today.

I have a dream that one day every valley shall be exalted, every hill and mountain shall be made low, the rough places will be made plain, and the crooked places will be made straight, and the glory of the Lord shall be revealed, and all flesh shall see it together.

This is our hope. This is the faith that I will go back to the South with. With this faith we will be able to hew out of the mountain of despair a stone of hope. With this faith we will be able to transform the jangling discords of our nation into a beautiful symphony of brotherhood.

With this faith we will be able to work together, to pray together, to struggle together, to go to jail together, to stand up for freedom together, knowing that we will be free one day.

This will be the day when all of God's children will be able to sing with new meaning, "My country 'tis of thee, sweet land of liberty, of thee I sing. Land where my fathers died, land of the Pilgrims' pride, from every mountainside, let freedom ring."

And if America is to be a great nation, this must become true. So let freedom ring from the prodigious hilltops of New Hampshire. Let freedom ring from the mighty mountains of New York. Let freedom ring from the heightening Alleghenies of Pennsylvania.

Let freedom ring from the snow-capped Rockies of Colorado. Let freedom ring from the curvaceous slopes of California. But not only that; let freedom ring from the Stone Mountain of Georgia. Let freedom ring from Lookout Mountain of Tennessee.

Let freedom ring from every hill and molehill of Mississippi. From every mountainside, let freedom ring.

And when this happens, and when we allow freedom ring, when we let it ring from every village and every hamlet, from every state and every city, we will be able to speed up that day when all of God's children, black men and white men, Jews and gentiles, Protestants and Catholics, will be able to join hands and sing in the words of the old Negro spiritual, "Free at last! Free at last! Thank God Almighty, we are free at last!"

Martin Luther had a great dream, but he didn't see its fulfillment in his lifetime. Imma hoped he would not suffer a similar fate.

During the following months at the bank in Benin admission letters from American graduate schools poured in, but Imma was crestfallen each time when the scholarship offer fell short. He went around with his head hanging down for days when he discovered that lower admission test scores undid him. Sleeping in the library doing additional preparation for GRE and GMAT had helped him succeed in the bank selection exam, but it had failed him in getting the scores to achieve his main goal.

Imma took a hard look at his savings account and mustered the courage to tell himself the truth. He had insufficient supplemental funds to convince the US consulate to give him a student visa. Going to America became a dream punted to some future.

3

Sit before you Recline

"Your attention please."

"May I *please* have your attention?"

Repeating himself with increasing volume, trying to balance courtesy with firmness, Luke didn't want to seem rude.

Someone clinked a spoon against a glass.

Silence.

"Thanks, everyone. And thanks to my friend with the spoon. She has taught me a lesson – it is not how loud the sound, but how right.

"We are so glad you could join us today to celebrate our friend and colleague, Imma Vine. The invitation said this occasion was for his birthday, but it has turned into a double-barrelled event. I am pleased to announce that Imma has just accepted a position at one of the best investment banks in the country, so we are also celebrating that tonight. Does this guy make us proud or what?"

"Yeah! Yeah! Yes he does!" People around the room applauded and cheered Imma's success.

Imma beamed with pride as they hugged him and patted his back. Some gave short speeches praising his accomplishments. His local and international awards testified to his brilliance, and now his single-minded devotion to work had been rewarded with career success. He rose to the occasion.

"I appreciate everyone for coming, and for your kind words. This is a cliché, but it is so true for me – it takes a village to raise a child. All of you, and many others who are not here, have played significant roles in what I have achieved in school and in my career. I am indebted to you for your sponsorships, for your friendships and encouragement, and for your understanding and indulgence when I made myself unavailable to socialize because I was in my room studying and chasing success.

"My parents are not here, but I would like to acknowledge them for the pride they take in me and my accomplishments. In particular, I can't let my mom down! As I head to the big city, Lagos, I assure you that I will pursue the *Golden Fleece* with every fibre of my being. I will not settle for less than the dream. Nothing else will satisfy. I promise to share the goodies with you all. You will not be forgotten. Thanks again!"

Since his compulsory one-year stint in the National Youth Service, Imma had worked two jobs. The investment bank job was the third. The commercial bank job was more financially rewarding and fulfilling than the teaching job. *Will the trend continue?*

Two weeks later, Imma started at Omega Merchant Bank, Lagos. Going through on-boarding in the posh meeting room at that first day, a new world open to Imma. He couldn't wait to plunge into his interesting corporate banking operations role and avail of the career growth opportunities. Awed at the sophisticated environment and high-class personnel, Imma bubbled with excitement. Before he left the office, he called his university classmate Chuma, now working in an Equipment Leasing company in Lagos, to join him at home after work for a little celebration.

Home and thanking his stars, Imma went into dreamland - again. *Big city, Big Boys and Girls Big bank, Big opportunities, Big bucks*. He vowed to not miss anything Lagos had to offer and pushed the American dream down his priority list – for now.

He fished out a left over champagne from the birthday party at Benin where his friends also sent him off to Lagos and awaited Chuma's arrival. Michael Jackson's *Don't Stop 'Til You Get Enough* was the most popular and danceable song at all the new students welcome and Christmas parties that 1979 when Imma entered the university. As he reminisced and danced to it all alone, he counted the years since that December 5, 1979 evening at the University of Nigeria.

Eight.

Even those many years later, IkeChi's offhand remark still hurt. Imma couldn't shake the embarrassment and shame of the "deprived" label. Unfortunately, IkeChi had been right, because Imma now recognized what his parents did to him by their inability to finance his education - Rejection. Child abuse. Failure to provide necessities for a child. He wasn't quite sure if that last one was legally accurate. *I don't care!* He shouted.

He danced harder, echoing the 'don't stop till you get enough' part.

As soon as Chuma arrived, Imma popped the champagne and they toasted to great success in Imma's career and their lives in Lagos.

Chuma noticed.

"Is this Michael Jackson song the only one you have?"

"There are others, but this one is very apt for the occasion," Imma said, laughing.

"How so?"

"It's been a long road getting here, man. I'm so thankful for this job, but there are miles to go yet."

"Long road to get here – what are you talking about?"

For the first time, Imma shared some of his agonizing story. "Chuma, I wasn't even supposed to be here, with a job like this. My parents couldn't even afford to register me for JAMB - the Joint Admissions Matriculation Board - university entrance examination."

"Really? So how did you get into our university – magic?"

"More or less. A miracle, I tell you. I thank God for my sister Chidubem's sacrifice to pay the paltry JAMB registration fee. I would not have survived the devastation of watching my classmates and friends take the examination without me."

"She paid your way through university too?"

Imma beckoned on him to sit down, and refilled their glasses.

"A greater miracle happened, and it's a long story. The only wealthy person from my village, Auntie Joanne, and her husband, provided the bulk of the finance. Succumbing to societal pressure to not educate females, her father refused to send her to teacher training college. My mom intervened, and through her influence Auntie Joanne's dad relented. She became a teacher and married Uncle Chuza, a successful businessman in Onitsha…"

"Was it because of them you did all your long vacation student jobs in Onitsha?"

"You remember – I did it in their transportation company and in some of the years in their home – teaching vacation classes to their kids." Imma continued the story.

"Both were lavish in their appreciation of Auntie Joanne's benefactor, my mom and they saw my university financing predicament as another payback opportunity. They gave me those vacation jobs and money to supplement whatever my family could eke out.

"Man, when I set foot on the University of Nigeria campus that day in September 1979, I was in a daze. And you can imagine how I felt that June in 1983 when I graduated."

"Wow, didn't know all that. And see where you are now – congratulations man!"

"Thanks Chuma. And I can't stop. Long ways to go!"

After five months as an investment banker, Imma had adorned his apartment with a wall-to-wall rug, leather upholstery, colourful drapes, and modern appliances. In Makurdi and Benin, his parking space had remained unoccupied, but now when Imma looked out the window he beamed at the sight of his 1985 Nissan Bluebird.

Twenty-six and unmarried, Imma's apartment buzzed during most weekends with up to eight people hanging out. The two spare bedrooms filled up most nights, and the living room accommodated the others, who made themselves comfortable on couches and the floor. Food and drink were always on the house. Most of Imma's home-town friends had not come as far as he had, and many of those who had made it to Lagos were still trying to find their footing. As the pacesetter, Imma did his best to provide inspiration and encouragement, sharing his good fortune with them and urging everyone up the success ladder. When a friend in medical school fell out with his father and lost his family financing, Imma chipped in to ensure that he achieved his dream of becoming a medical doctor.

Now owning a car, Imma visited his Umunumo rural home town more often. Singing and dancing greeted him the first time he drove into the family compound. As people peered through the windows, Imma proudly flung open the doors and urged them to take a seat. Beaming with smiles and acknowledging the congratulatory messages, his parents treated the people to snacks and drinks. Imma sank into a chair and watched as the villagers took turns sitting in the car. *The people's car.*

The next day he proudly helped his mother into the passenger's seat – the *owner's seat*, he announced, with a grin – and drove her to the market. On their return he drove Papa to visit his two sisters in neighbouring towns, happy to relieve him of the long bicycle ride.

Making his rounds to visit village families, Imma listened to an earful of complaints. Insufficient funds to get medical treatment topped them all. Their continued reliance on traditional medicine and self-medication gave him great concern. When a doctor he knew from university established a nearby clinic, Imma signed a retainer agreement to treat the poor from his village and put the charges on his account.

While relishing in the respect and acceptance that came from helping people, Imma was jolted to reality by his no-nonsense mom who sat him down, gave him a lecture on money management, and urged him to get his priorities right.

"The father of my husband, you have to sit before you recline."

"What does that mean?"

"My son, I see you are being generous and doing all this charity. I hear your house in Lagos is like a free-for-all hotel. But you are just starting life, and you cannot solve everybody's problems. Trying to recline when you are not yet seated can only lead to a bad fall."

"I'm not solving everybody's problems. Just trying to help where I can."

"It's a good thing, and you probably got that from me. However, my priorities were properly ordered."

Imma listened carefully as Mama counted on her fingers.

"One, you have younger siblings and relations to help with sponsoring their education.

"Two, you don't own a house. How long do you want to continue to give your money to someone else, paying those high city rents?

"Three, will you live in this house your father and I built forever? When will you start thinking of building a good country home?

"Four, is it not time to make preparation for getting married? Marrying is not cheap.

"My son, you need to start saving money for all these things. Don't seek popularity at the expense of your priorities."

She put her hands lovingly on his shoulders, and left the room.

That night, Imma stared at the ceiling for a long while, forced into deep assessment. Alarm bells rang when he discovered that he was spending almost 100% of his earnings. His only savings were the little amount he had put away in his previous job. Mama hadn't even included graduate studies in America on her list. If only she knew – graduate studies was still Imma's number-one priority.

He made a decision to start budgeting and putting money away. He smiled as he went through Mama's list again. Number four was getting married. Imma amused himself by imagining who was on her list of girls for him. *At the top of Mama's qualifying traits for the girl would be, 'very strong and likes farming'.* Mama's view was that Imma's home would be a disaster if he married a woman as lazy as him, and she never failed to try to push him into farming.

Imma hated farming, and relished the accomplishment of escaping that.

4

Chasing after the Wind

Imma let out a sigh as his Nissan Bluebird rustled through the carpet of fallen leaves and came to a stop in his driveway. The tall palms, conifers and eucalyptus trees at the corners of the fence swayed and whispered in the evening wind. The laughter of nearby kids announced that Imma's neighbours were back from their trip. He sat in his car, debating whether to go over as usual and say hello before mounting the stairs up to his apartment. Not today, he decided.

Yawning, he noticed the groceries on the back seat. "They can wait till tomorrow," he thought. Taking a deep breath, he lugged his work bag and a few binders upstairs. Music boomed from an outdoor event somewhere down the street, and Imma was grateful that the sound drowned out the pounding in his rib cage. Letting himself in, he flipped on the air conditioning and dropped to the couch, shoes and all. He longed for the distraction of the television, but the remote was a few feet away and he couldn't muster enough strength to get up. When he turned the other way the kitchen came into view. "Dinner is the least of my concerns right now," he thought, stretching out on the couch and staring at the ceiling.

The wall clock chimed. It had been an hour since he lay down, and he was still awake. Imma calculated that that was about fifty-five minutes longer than his average time to fall asleep. Feeling dampness, he unbuttoned his shirt.

That day at Beta Investment Bank, his six-month probation period performance review had gone well.

"Imma, everyone is happy with your work so far, and your appointment has been confirmed," his manager, Mr. Adelana Oluwaseyi, said. "Congratulations!"

"Thank you sir. That's really good news!"

"Based on your CEP and the career development plan that has been created for you, we see you making the manager position in about a year."

"What's CEP, sir?"

Adelana invited him to a white board at the corner of the office and drew some graphs and scenarios.

"CEP is currently estimated potential. Our performance and progression management system measures each staff member's capacity to assume higher responsibilities. I can share that you currently score very well."

"I'm so glad to hear that, and I appreciate the support from everyone."

"Note the key word 'currently'. It is a live tracker. What happens in six months or a year depends on how your performance rates against your potential."

"I'll do my best, sir."

The traffic had been bumper to bumper driving home, but Imma had weathered worse in the six months living in Lagos. It was not the traffic.

What's wrong with me?

Imma sprang up at the sound of the doorbell. *Oh, no – not today.* He lay back down. Ignoring the second ring, hoping the person would go away, was futile. Two minutes later, a blare. Whoever was at the door was not going away. Imma went to the door, and as he leaned toward the peephole a voice rang out.

"Son of Vine, open the door, man!"

LuChi Chidi Shepherd! Unmistakable. No one else called Imma by that nickname.

"Son of Shepherd!" Imma flung the door open. Bear hugs.

"Good to see you, man. Have been meaning to connect since you joined us in Lagos, but man, just too much hustle. Congrats on the job. You have joined the big boys; you have arrived. God is good!"

Imma started to respond to the compliment, but LuChi chattered on. "There better be food in this bachelor house, 'cause I'm starving. Need energy for the catch-up tonight. My apartment is very far from here. Even if it was not, I plan on crashing here tonight; lots to talk about. Moreover, I hear you got a nice abode here but I gotta confirm for myself. Didn't they say the proof of the pudding is in the eating?" LuChi laughed.

LuChi. One of the nicest young men Imma knew. He felt privileged to call LuChi a close friend.

Living in separate cities for university and work, they had seen each other recently only once - two years ago at LuChi's graduation ceremony. Living in a country where a personal telephone was a luxury only the rich enjoyed, neither friend had one, so no phone visits. Imma missed the camaraderie they had enjoyed growing up and while attending secondary school vacation classes together.

It would be a long night indeed. Alone time was the prescription Imma had given himself to reflect on the gloom, agitation, and low energy that had engulfed him for the past few weeks, but if anybody could make him feel better, it would be LuChi.

"So how has it been, your commercial bank job in Benin compared to your investment bank job in the big city?" LuChi asked as they foraged in the pantry and fridge for some dinner.

"Not bad. I've been really fortunate to make some progress, particularly with this new job. And quite thankful. You probably heard that our town's attorney, Chris, referred me. He is a personal lawyer to the chairman of the bank, and that referral got me the written job test opportunity. I did well enough on the test and interview, but honestly, being the chairman's candidate must have swayed it in my favour. Given the attractiveness of this job, there were many candidates. I don't want to kid myself into thinking that I am smarter than those who were not selected.

"As for the commercial bank and investment bank, and small city versus big-city differences, it's like night and day. But there are miles to go. Miles to go!"

"Son of Vine, we are thankful for Uncle Chris, but have no doubt in your own abilities. With or without that referral, you would have been selected on your merit. Didn't I hear that Chris referred two of you to the bank chairman, but the other person wasn't selected? We know how you got into your previous bank job, don't we? You came tops out of more than two thousand others in the aptitude test. You showed them what a small-town boy can do," LuChi smiled, letting out another laugh.

"It was just good luck."

"What are you saying? Your selection was not luck, my brother. God is good to you! Oh yes, I know He is – and you better know it, too. Chris and the bank chairman were just vessels God used, and your intelligence is His gift to you. Those are all manifestations of His goodness to you. And that requires an appropriate response from you."

Imma tried to process where LuChi was going with this God thing. He started to respond, but LuChi just continued talking.

"Son of Vine, the Lord has been good to me, too! It's not been easy and certainly not as rosy. But He has been good! I got my degree, and although it took a few years of hustle I've landed a job at *The Flagship* newspaper to pursue a career in journalism. The pay is only entry level, and nothing compared to what commercial and investment banks offer. I don't have a nice apartment like you. Yet. In fact, I've moved from place to place to find affordable accommodation; where I live now is a budget one-room joint in the low-income part of the city. But, boy, am I grateful! It's just a place to sleep, sometimes only a few nights a month. As you know, my job involves a lot of country-wide travel in the hunt for breaking news and interviews."

LuChi had studied Languages in university. And since learning that he had joined *The Guardian*, Imma had become a daily patron. Not because *The Guardian* was the best, but because his close friend worked there. "That's why," Imma mused.

The LuChi he knew was nice and warm. On the gentle side, but driven and ambitious. But this was a different LuChi. How could anyone living in a shack with a low-paying job be so passionate, excited and joyful?

"Son of Shepherd, I hear you. It's not bad that you are writing for *The Guardian*. But you must not settle. We need to continually advance. Whatever you may say about how well you think I've done, where I am is certainly far from where I need to be. No, I haven't arrived. There are still many more rungs of the corporate ladder to climb. There are still those promises – obligations – to fulfill for my mother. You know, building my country home, getting married, giving her some grandchildren, owning a home in the city – all that. The dream life beckons, and there'll be no happiness, peace, or fulfillment for me until all those boxes are checked."

LuChi smiled. "I need a drink." He went to the kitchen area and opened a few cabinets in search of a glass.

"Do you run a pharmacy here?" LuChi had stumbled on Imma's cache of energy-booster drinks, mood-boosters, tranquilizers and more. He took a long, piercing look at his friend.

"Oh, those. Yeah, I've been a bit under the weather."

"I'm not a doctor, but I don't believe the drugs I see here are for a-bit-under-the-weather health issues."

"It's not what you think."

"So what is it? You look beat, man!"

"I've seen two specialists and they have done a few tests, but they can't seem to find out what's wrong. I don't know. But chasing the dream can be a lot of pressure. Those boxes need to be checked…"

"Son of Vine, so you are not content, even with how far you've come?"

"Far from it."

"So when will you be content? When you climb the corporate ladder and acquire more stuff?"

"Certainly."

"Son of Vine, that's a lot of pressure on yourself. A recipe to be sick. I doubt that climbing the success ladder will give you the fulfillment you need, though."

"Look, son of Shepherd, you know my story growing up. What you may not know is that I made a vow that neither I nor anyone in my family will suffer deprivation again!"

"Wow, I didn't know that."

"Now you know."

"Yes, and I can appreciate that. And you should be proud of yourself for how far your family has come."

"Still miles to go."

"I share in your aspiration to help lift us and our families out of poverty – what you call deprivation. But I'm wondering if the issue is not another kind of deprivation, one that success and getting rich, as good as they are, may not cure."

"What do you mean?"

"Let me tell you. I'm grateful for where I am and for what I have. But my fulfillment and joy are not based on things. They wouldn't even be based on my becoming editor of *The Flagship* with much higher pay and a posh apartment. In fact, if I lost this job or got a lower paying one, and had to move into a smaller shack or sleep in someone's living room, the fulfillment and joy I've received would not be taken away."

Imma frowned. "It saddens me that you have settled for less, but appear happy and at peace while doing so."

"I am sorry to disappoint you. Dreams change, you know. And mine certainly has. Let me tell you the full story. And have some more coffee. I don't want you dozing off."

LuChi excused himself for a bathroom break. When he returned, he grabbed an apple and continued.

"I met Jesus Christ a year ago. He was introduced to me by a friend."

"What do you mean?" Imma interrupted. "We've known Jesus since we were kids."

"What I mean is knowing Him personally. My friend shared the news of what Jesus came to bring to the world and to each individual. *Personally*. Remember the story of how angels spoke to the shepherds at night? 'I'm here to bring you good news,' they said. 'News of great joy for all people in the world. Today in Bethlehem a Saviour has been born for you. Glory to God in Heaven, and on earth peace and goodwill toward men.'

"Then there was the personal introduction to the wise men from the East, who testified, 'we have seen His star and have come to worship Him.' The star led them all the way to the house where Jesus lay. Overjoyed, they bowed down and worshipped Him. Unpacking their bags, they gave Jesus gifts of gold, frankincense, and myrrh.

"Son of Vine, the shepherds found Him just as they were told. The wise men too. People representing the lowest and the highest. Filled with peace and joy, they were never the same. As they say, 'Wise people still seek Jesus.' So you should not be surprised that I sought and found Jesus personally. I got wise," he quipped, laughing.

Imma sat still, befuddled. LuChi took another bite at his apple and continued.

"That's it. I have met and asked Him into my heart. He now lives in me. The same joy, peace, and goodwill He brought to all who heard and believed in Him find their expression in my own life. And quite independent of what I have or don't have – job, material stuff, and all that."

"Good for you," Imma said, politely dismissing his friend.

"Son of Vine, show me my room and go to bed. Enough catch-up for tonight. Been a long day for me. Neither of us is made of wood, and this flesh needs some rest.

"And think of what I said: God's goodness to you requires an appropriate response."

Clearing up, Imma pondered LuChi's story. Did his parents know about his strange new personal relationship with Jesus? Making his way to the guestroom, Imma was greeted with LuChi's snoring. He turned off the light, gently closed the door, and headed to his own room.

Respond appropriately to God's goodness.

What does that even mean?

5

Crossroads

Imma squinted as a glint of light reflected on the large mirror in his room. Lingering on the bed, he replayed last night's chat with LuChi.

LuChi knocked on his door. "Son of Vine, ain't you awake yet? It's 11 am already! Even though it's Saturday, we can't sleep all day."

Last night wasn't a dream. LuChi, the new LuChi, indeed had visited, and is still in Imma's home.

Imma came out of his room, yawning and stretching.

"Good morning, Son of Shepherd. Trust you were comfortable."

"For sure. Now that I've fully tasted your place I can testify that this is a great abode you have here. Great experience worth repeating. Now I have a second home in the city, and you are going to be seeing lots of me!" LuChi let out another big laugh.

"Not a problem -- you are welcome any time. I'd like to come know your home as well. Your home is also my home."

Getting breakfast ready, Imma handed LuChi a cup of tea. "I thought I was the only guy who snores!"

"I snore?" LuChi chuckled. "The friend I shared my room with alleged the same but I didn't believe him. I told him I sometimes hum and sing in my sleep and he just mistook those sounds for snoring. That's how tired I was, though. Drifted off without reading my Bible and praying. Anyway, whatever you do, don't tell Tessie! Don't want any snoring tales to stop her from giving me my 'Yes, I do...' She will have to find out that I snore on our honeymoon – and then it will be too late."

"Who's Tessie? Wow, you have more to tell me. And talking about the three sweetest words any guy wants to hear, I have my own story, too. But first, this 'appropriate response' thing from last night…"

"Oh, that," LuChi said. "God does good to people who do not know or care about Him; and He shows kindness to those who think they are bad and unworthy. His desire is that such goodness will lead them to repentance. Meaning, to know that 'God is *for* me, not against me.'

"Imma, He has been good to you, as we all know. The response He requires from you is to change your life, your old way of thinking, and turn to seeking His purpose for your life. I have done that. That's how I asked Jesus into my life, to be my Saviour and Lord. And that's why I have the joy, peace and strength that flow from the inside. Let me tell you another story."

Imma's eyes caught a thin cloud of smoke coming from the cooker. "The eggs!" He quickly turned off the stove.

"A good time to break. Or rather, let's have this story over breakfast." As they ate, LuChi regaled him with more stories.

"There was this guy, blind from birth, who begged on the streets for sustenance. Jesus met and healed him, but he didn't have any idea who Jesus was. As people argued about who performed the healing, the healed man shunned all the controversy. He just acknowledged the goodness that had been done to him. 'All I know is that I was blind, and now I can see.' Meeting Jesus later, he worshipped Him and became His follower.

"Son of Vine, one more, and then I gotta go home, man.

"This other guy, his name was Zacchaeus. Let's call him Zacch. Zacch was the chief tax collector in the region and had become rich. He was one of the most loathed people in the land because not only did he collect tax on behalf of the Romans who ruled and oppressed his people, he was also believed to have exacted more from the people to enrich himself.

"Zacch sought to see Jesus as He passed along the streets, but being a short man he was handicapped to see through the crowd that always surrounded Jesus. One day, piqued by curiosity and shunning ridicule, Zacch clambered up a tree beside the road. Granting more than he wished, Jesus called him down and went for dinner in his home. Thus, Zacch received the greatest honour Jesus could bestow in that era: a visit to an individual's home! There was no condemnation for all the evil that Zacch had done; just love and mercy. Filled with both remorse and great joy, Zacch promised to give half of his wealth to the poor, and to pay back many times over what he had cheated people of. In response, Jesus announced, 'salvation has come to this home today, for I came to seek and save those who are lost.'

"There again, God's goodness led this man to repentance, turning from the pursuit of riches to following the will of God."

As they got into the car to drop off LuChi at the bus stop, both instinctively held their noses.

The groceries from yesterday!

"What's that?"

"Must be the meat I bought yesterday. I did some grocery shopping on my way home from work…"

"You forgot groceries in the car? And we were scrounging for dinner last night!"

"Son of Shepherd, I didn't forget. I was just too drained to bother taking them upstairs. I really need to find a solution to…"
"I've already told you the solution, the permanent solution. The question is, when are you going to listen? I'll be praying for you: the joy of the Lord is your strength."

On their way to the bus stop, LuChi broke the silence. "I almost forgot: you know that Nath is here, right? He moved here about a year ago, after me. You both have become my running mates, chasing me to this big city. I'm glad we're all here now. God sure has a plan."

"Nath is here? We've been out of touch for a while."

"So you didn't hear what happened to him?"

"What? Is he okay?"

They arrived at the bus stop. "The bus is leaving," LuChi said, running off. "I will let Nath know you are here."

Nathaniel (Nath) UkaChi Gate. A close friend that Imma and LuChi shared.

Nath the Bulldozer. What happened to Nath? Is he okay?

The week inched along. Battling with the turmoil of LuChi's visit, Imma eagerly waited for Saturday to visit Nath. Comparing his accomplishments with those of LuChi, Imma shuddered at the irony of LuChi being happier and more fulfilled than Imma himself. He fought to dismiss LuChi's new personal relationship with Jesus, concluding that it was just a copout. *LuChi has found a clever way to rationalize his failure to pursue the dream.* On his way to Nath's home, Imma was happy for the opportunity to run these things by his old friend.

Weaving, his tires splashing water from potholes he couldn't avoid, Imma heard cursing from wet people wiping their faces. Waving his apologies, Imma drove slower, stopping a few times to ask for directions – only to find to his chagrin that some of the people he had thanked for helping had sent him in the wrong direction.

Imma caught himself cursing those who had cruelly misled him. *Why don't people admit they don't know?*

He parked, studying the route description and landmarks, surveying the grey buildings dotting both sides of the road – everything from grocery stores to motels, all with bold signs. He was lost. The sun was now red hot, with children running around playing and laughing. Imma wished he could exchange places with them. Hitting the steering hard with both fists and wincing, he saw a guy walking on the other side of the street. He looked closely. Nath!

Imma couldn't miss the gait. As he drove closer Nath kept walking away, as if to avoid being hit by this seemingly inattentive driver.

"Have you developed car-phobia, or what?" Imma twisted his face as he stopped next to Nath.

"Imma! Is that you? Son of his father! Oh my goodness! Imma Vine?"

Imma jumped out of the car and into the huge embrace of his friend. Nath had his own pet name for Imma. *Son of his father.*

"Nath the Bulldozer! Who else would risk trying to run you down on the sidewalk?"

Nath was a big, muscular guy who pulled no punches.

"That's right; it would be a huge mistake. Let me correct that: in my former life, it would be a big provocation." Nath laughed.

As they drove, Nath said, "The Holy Spirit told me to come and fetch you from the street where you would be wandering, looking for my house."

"Holy Spirit. Really?"

"Really."

"That's creepy."

Ignoring that, Nath laughed again. "What He didn't tell me, though, was that the hunter would be the hunted. Instead of me finding you, you would find me and almost run me into the gutter."

Alarm bells went off for Imma. *Since when did the Holy Spirit start talking to Nath?*

Nath surveyed the interior of his friend's car.

"You are looking good, man! And this car. Wow. Haven't you arrived?"

"I've been fortunate. I can't complain too much."

"Oh, so you can complain some? I don't own a car. I may not be looking as good as you, but I have no complaints."

Nath opened the door, and bellowed. "Welcome to my humble abode of love and peace."

"Thank you, Nath. Glad to be here."

Imma surveyed the one-room apartment, seeing only a reading table and two chairs for furniture. The room was hot and humid, with no air conditioner and a fan that just spread the hot air. But he also saw colourful wallpaper, calendars, and posters that breathed life and beauty into the space. Imma was glad for the soft music drifting from a corner... just what he needed to soothe his jarred nerves.

"Make yourself comfortable. I prepared your favourite dish. And there's lots of drinks. Soft drinks. This reunion is worth celebrating."

Inhaling the familiar aroma, Imma's mouth watered for the steamed rice, fried plantain, with *okporoko* (stockfish) and goat meat stew – red with lots of tomato! Digging in, they chattered on.

"LuChi told me about his visit with you. Congratulations on the great strides you have made – the Big Boys job, the great accommodation, the plans for a country home, marriage, all that to make your mom happy, I hear."

"Oh, good that LuChi shared with you. We had a whole night and the next morning to catch up. Yes, I've made modest strides and won some awards. But miles to go… many miles to go, man."

"Yeah, the awards. In fact, the last time I saw you was on TV, receiving first prize for the Martin Luther King Jr. essay contest. You made us proud, man!"

"Thank you so much. Wow, it's really been a long time since we last saw each other."

Nath shared his journey since their last meeting. He had graduated with a business degree. Two years ago he had completed his one-year voluntary service and moved to the city in search of work. So far he had only found a stop-gap job, but it put food on the table and financed his professional designation studies. Completing the professional exam was taking longer than he liked, but he was plugging on.

"I am a Believer, so I cannot do anything but believe. I have complete peace about it," Nath concluded with a sunny smile.

"That's quite the faith. Good for you. I wouldn't trust myself to exhibit such faith in your situation," Imma said, grimacing.

"LuChi asked me if I had heard what happened to you. He was rushing off to board the bus, so he didn't get a chance to tell me. What was he talking about? What happened to you? He really frightened me, as I'd imagined the worst."

"LuChi! I'm sure he didn't mean to frighten you – he probably just wanted to whet your appetite to see me. And he succeeded! In just one week, here you are," Nath said, laughing.

"But seriously, a few major things have happened to me. I wonder which one LuChi was alluding to?"

"Tell me all of them, since they are few. We have enough time."

Nath shared stories about his heartache from the breakup with his high school sweetheart, Rose. Theirs had been a real-life version of the Shakespearean Romeo and Juliet story, without the tragedy.

"What, Rose and you are no longer together? Unbelievable! What happened?"

"She somehow managed to see the trajectory of my life, and she didn't think I would be ready to settle down as soon as she wanted. She met another man, and guess what? They are already engaged. Won't be surprised if you get her wedding invitation shortly."

"Oh, Nath, I'm so sorry to hear that. Who would have believed that Rose could do that to you? To us? She didn't consider the love and friendship we lavished on her. They better not send me a wedding invite. Nath Gate not the groom? I ain't going!"

"I can understand your disappointment..."

"You do? But I don't get it – you don't seem disappointed. Two years since graduation, you still haven't found a regular job, and Rose left you for another guy. Yet you say you have no complaints. That looks like an ostrich with its head in the sand to me!"

"Imma, you are a best friend. I really appreciate that you care. But truly, I'm good; not pretending. I've got over the breakup with Rosy."

Rosy. That was the name Nath and his friends called her. Imma had called her Rose to press home his disapproval. But Nath still called her Rosy.

"You shouldn't judge her harshly. After all, you haven't heard her side of the story. Don't be such a short fuse!" Nath laughed.

"Let me clarify what I mean by having no complaints. I have ample opportunity for complaints, but I just don't take them. I take a pass. I turn them into opportunity for prayer, with thanksgiving, to the One who promised me that all things will work together for my good because I love Him and I'm walking in His purpose. As you know, it hasn't always been like that for me. It's been three years since I gave my life to Jesus Christ. Perhaps that's the other thing LuChi was alluding to when he asked if you had heard what happened to me?"

"You did what?"

"I made Jesus Christ my personal Saviour and Lord," Nath explained, smiling broadly. "A lady I knew in university shared the good news of Jesus Christ in a way I had never understood it before. How He came to give us the God-Life that is unending and abundant."

"Nath, I know about Jesus and God," Imma cut in. "And I know the life I want and how to pursue it."

"I'm aware that you know about Jesus Christ. I did, too. But this is different. This is about knowing Him personally in your heart. For example, I now know Him personally as the *Prince of Peace*. And having entered into a personal relationship with Him, He lives in me. My faith in Him and His Peace now mark my life and help me to overcome every disappointment and every heartache. I truly have no complaints anymore. I still have loss and disappointment; it's just that I have new strength. I am differently equipped, if you like, to deal with them. Peace is not the absence of storms. Rather it is calmness, faith, and hope – even in the midst of storms."

Imma picked up a magazine on the table and lazily flipped through. Nath could have been speaking to himself.

"I hear you concerning the life you are pursuing. Keep an open mind. You never know, that life and the path to it could be quite different from what we dreamed of growing up."

Looking at his watch, Nath said, "I have an event in an hour, but you are welcome to join us. Otherwise, you can just drop me off; it's on your way home."

Imma changed his mind about the questions he had for Nath around LuChi and his new lifestyle. Nath did not sound any different from LuChi.

"What event?"

"It's an open-air program to share the good news of Jesus Christ, trusting that others will consider entering into a personal relationship with Him as well. LuChi should be there, too."

"Looks like it's going to rain."

"We believe that the rain will hold its peace through the program. But even if it doesn't, it will be showers of blessing. The program will continue," Nath replied, brimming over with confidence.

What boldness. Stop rain by faith? In all Imma's life he had never heard of such a thing. If anything, the cultural practice in many parts of Nigeria was to pay native rainmakers who were thought to have the power to divert rain.

"I can drop you there."

Getting up, Imma said, "Nath you may not complain, but I do. Your apartment can use some comfortable furniture, man. At least one soft couch for your guests. Those chairs are quite harsh on the backside, man."

"I'm not complaining. And great that you mentioned it. I've already paid for furniture for the new accommodation I'm looking for. The furniture guy has been after me to take delivery. LuChi mentioned your apartment is spacious. Can I keep my furniture with you till I get a new place?"

"Sure. Feel free to bring it over anytime."

LuChi was already there when they arrived at Nath's event. Imma didn't have anything particular to do at home, so he decided out of curiosity to stay.

As they set up the stage and chairs, it started to drizzle. The organizers, including Nath and LuChi, went out commanding the rain to stop. Imma stayed in the shelter and watched. *Let me see how they stop the elements by shouting at the clouds.*

The rain fell for a short time, then stopped, but not before his friends and their associates got drenched, still smiling, as they prayed and sang. No complaints. No escape to shelter.

Did the rain stop on its own? Or in response to their faith?

The program ended, and Imma offered to drop off Nath and LuChi.

"Son of Vine, nice to see you again," said LuChi. "Glad you joined us for this program. I pray you were blessed. Did Nath tell you what happened to him?"

"Yes, he did. I've been so upset with Rose. Son of Shepherd, can you imagine? All that we invested in Rose – the travels to accompany Nath to see her, combining our meagre savings to buy her expensive gifts? And Nath tells me it's okay; he has no complaints."

"That's correct," said Nath. "I joked with Imma earlier that in my former life it would have been a huge mistake for someone to try to piss me off – but that's because the Nath that Imma used to know has died. That's the part I didn't tell him about Rosy.

"She found out that I had accepted Jesus into my life, and she decided the old Nath had died. She reached the conclusion that this new Nath wasn't the one she had fallen in love with. I encouraged her to enter same personal relationship with Jesus, to taste the new life, but she would have none of it. The old Nath has died, been buried, and is never rising up again."

"Let's forgive and forget Rosy for now," LuChi interjected. "Thankfully, the Lord is doing new things and giving us new friends. There's my friend Tessie. Imma, you indicated that there's someone? And Nath, have you found the one yet? The right one, as obviously Rosy wasn't for you."

"I agree with LuChi," said Nath. "As I've told you, Imma, the breakup with Rosy wasn't the only thing that happened to me. Before that, Jesus happened to me."

Imma cherry-picked, playing deaf to all the Jesus talk. "LuChi, I want to hear about Tessie! When I meet her, the first thing I'm going to let her know is that you snore. A lot. In the interest of full disclosure," Imma said, laughing. "As for my heartthrob, Gift, it's a little complicated...."

6

Strange Friends, Narrow Path

"Am I the only one hungry? Imma, there's a restaurant around the corner. Turn in and let's have some food – I want to hear about Gift, and it will be sweeter over a delicious meal. You are both bachelors like me, with no one to rush home to."

Did the change affect his appetite, too? "LuChi, where does all that food go? You're still as skinny as ever."

"Better to be growing vertically than horizontally."

Imma and Nath turned to each other. There was no point trying to dissuade LuChi. "We concede: it must take a lot of food to be a six-footer."

On the next street a bright neon sign swayed in the light wind, inviting them in bold letters to *Flavour's Cuisine*.

"Their food better be good!" Nath quipped.

LuChi did not have to respond to that. As they entered the restaurant, a rich aroma of freshly cooked rice, beans, plantain and soup as well as assorted meats sizzling on the barbeque waltzed into their nostrils.

Settled down to their meal, Imma brought back his request. "LuChi, now let's hear about Tessie. Start from the beginning."

"My friend Tessie! I'm not shy at all to talk about her."

They had met at their Fellowship place and served together in the prayer and hospitality teams. Tessie was a devout young woman who had met Jesus Christ in university. Over many months of Fellowshipping and serving together, LuChi began to like her very much. Initially just as a sister in the Lord, with no ulterior motives. Tessie was single-minded in her devotion to her faith, and her countenance discouraged any ideas of a dating relationship. Worse, LuChi found out that she was irritated by his restless personality – his hardly-can-sit-down, always-on-the-move, always-serving nature.

"To cut the story short, she could not resist my special attention and friendliness for too long. Our relationship morphed from co-worshippers and team members to friends. Very good friends. Given our commitment to the Lord, we have decided to separately pray about whether it is in His perfect will for us to spend our lives together. That's where we are right now. If we both get the yes, we will start dating."

"I like her already," said Imma.

"She is a lovely young lady," affirmed Nath. "I attend the same Fellowship with LuChi and Tessie. If the Holy Spirit gives the green light, they will be the best and sweetest God-loving couple you ever saw – Tessie's toughness notwithstanding. We sometimes call her Margaret Thatcher. You know the tough British prime minister? They are of similar mould. Tough in a good way. I don't have any experience, but haven't you heard that nothing softens a woman like love and romance? I know LuChi will saturate her in love. Not sure about the romance part, though. He has no experience with that – as far as I know," Nath said, chuckling.

"No experience with romance should be no problem," Imma said. "It can be learned and, as they say, practice makes perfect. LuChi, you are of age. Speak for yourself: did you have some experience in the years we've been apart? I actually did see some girls hanging around when I came for your graduation. Those girls you introduced as friends, classmates, or whatever – did you get romantically involved with anyone?"

"Oh no, not at all," replied LuChi. "I was focused on my studies. Given the number of siblings my parents financed through school, I had to ensure I completed my program quickly to relieve them of the burden. Dating would have been a distraction."

"Ok, got it. We believe you. At least now we know our job: we will remind you to learn romance if you are going to get married. Otherwise, as Nath has suggested, you won't survive this Margaret Thatcher you call Tessie.

"Anyway, I want to meet her. When is she coming to your home? I can plan my next visit for the same day."

"She doesn't come to my home, and I don't go to hers. Not yet. You will have to meet her at one of our Church events."

"What do you mean, you don't visit each other at home?"

"When you meet Jesus Christ and enter into a personal relationship with Him as your Saviour and Lord, there is a new code of conduct," Nath explained. "We value purity in our human relationships, and one of the ways we do that in opposite-gender friendships is to ban meetings alone in private places like homes."

"You are telling me that all the guys and gals in your Church do not get to test their would-be spouses before making the major commitment? Before tying the knot and losing your freedom forever?"

"That's why people need to pray and ensure they have heard from God that they are meant for each other. Sleeping together before the wedding, before marriage, is no test or guarantee of anything. Knowing that you love each other purely and are meant for each other is all that matters."

"So your Church is trying to produce more Virgin Mary's?"

"Jesus fills you with pure love, and the power to live in purity. He wipes out your past, and it becomes a new journey of abstinence if single, and of fidelity to your spouse if married."

"Son of Vine, what Nath said about followers of Jesus having a new code of conduct and value system is true," said LuChi. "We are in a new kingdom – God's Kingdom – and the constitution and laws, if you like, are different. The way to describe the transition is that we died to our old ways and must now live by the new. Purity and abstinence before marriage are values we treasure. I ain't touching my friend Tessie before marriage. Or any other woman. It's the right, respectful and honourable thing to do."

"I don't get it. When you met Jesus you died?"

"Yes. That's the reality. There has to be death of the old before there can be birth of the new."

"In that case you people may remain my friends, but I will have none of your Jesus thing. I don't want to die!"

"Son of Vine, don't rush into any such decision. If we are your friends, will we find something good and not share it with you? All we are doing is trying to make you understand the pathway to the best prosperous life you can have. The life of love, joy, peace, goodness, divine health, the miraculous, and fulfillment that only a personal relationship with Jesus can bring."

"True. And son of his father, you would need to start reading the Bible, as LuChi and I now do. Sad that in our old life we were not encouraged to read God's Word for ourselves. Otherwise you would have seen, as we now have, the requirement that says except a grain of wheat falls to the ground and dies, it would not have the new life that is fruitful and multiplying. We don't have to weep over our old, dead life. The new life from Jesus Christ is delightfully awesome and fruitful! In fact, Jesus warned that the people who love their old life in this world will miss true life, but those who detach their lives from this world and seek Him above all will find true life and enjoy it forever."

"I am sorry," said Imma, "but this Jesus talk has gotten me confused. We were all doing well in our religion. I don't understand this new fanaticism with having a personal relationship with Jesus."

"It depends on what you mean by doing well. It's not just about success and material wealth. It's about the kind of life that includes fulfillment and contentment, joy and peace. Imma, we had this chat in your home regarding your cache of medicines…"

"LuChi, that's below the belt."

"Respectfully, you have to wonder why, with all you have accomplished and acquired, you seem to be restless and unfulfilled, to the point of feeling sick."

"Son of his father, it's by faith in Jesus who loves us and sacrificed Himself for us. I know it is a lot to take in right now. You will get it in time, don't worry."
"And how did your parents react to your embrace of this fanaticism? My family will crucify me, especially my mom. She won't hear of it."

"We are adults and can make our own decisions. Moreover…."

"Enough, men!" interjected LuChi. "Time to go; getting late. As you know, my apartment is far away. Or is Imma trying to keep us here so late that I'll be forced to crash at his abode again? No way; I need to be home. Things I need for Church tomorrow morning are all there. And I'll be late if I have to first go from your place to my home in the morning."

"Before we leave, when do I get to meet Tessie?"

"We have a program next Saturday evening at our Fellowship place. You should come. And bring Gift."

"Yes, I agree! Come with Gift, and we all can meet there."

"I'll check with her. As for me, it seems that's my earliest opportunity to meet Tessie, so I'll take it. I'm also curious to see your Fellowship and what you do there. But if that's where you all met Jesus and died, don't have any illusions. I'm not coming to die!"

Driving to LuChi's and Nath's Fellowship place, Gift was excited to meet Imma's best friends.

"I must warn you, those two guys are not the same friends I knew a few years ago."

"How do you mean?"

"They have changed. They have been talking about entering into a personal relationship with Jesus Christ. They say the LuChi and Nath I knew have *died*. Crazy, isn't it?"

"Interesting."

"No, weird. These are guys I have known most of my life, and with whom I shared my aspirations of the dream life – climbing the corporate ladder, owning luxury cars and homes, and landing the most beautiful women like you. You know what I mean? But now they seem to have lowered their sights, and seemingly with no complaints."

"Are you judging your friends?"

"They had so much promise. We had ambitions for much more, but they appear to be settling for less. That would be such a waste. That's all I'm saying."

"Is this about losing the friends you knew, or about their change of ambition?"

"Both."

"You're a nice guy then, considering."

"Considering what?"

"Considering that you are going to their Fellowship place."

"I'm curious, that's all. And I want to meet Tessie."

"Who is Tessie?"

Waving and running, LuChi directed Imma to a parking lot with Nath and a lady following behind.

That must be Tessie.

Light-skinned, average height, very pretty and smiling, she hugged Gift and Imma.

They all went into the Church to be introduced. Fellowship started, and Imma quietly observed while Gift joined in the animated singing, clapping, dancing, and praying. The leader of the Fellowship said he would tell a story.
-

- *Jesus had a cousin, John by name. John was also a teacher and had followers called disciples. One day as he was visiting with two of the disciples, John saw Jesus walking by.*
-
- *"Look, that's Him! That is the Lamb of God! The One who God has sent as the ultimate sacrifice for the cleansing of our sins!"*
-
- *Curious, the two ran to Jesus.*
-
- *"What do you want?" Jesus asked.*
-
- *"We would like to know where you live, and we want to get to know you. We don't quite understand what our master, John, is saying about you."*
-
- *"Come and see," Jesus replied. They ended up spending the rest of the day with Him.*
  -
- *One of the two disciples was named Andrew. He rushed to tell his brother, Simon, that they had found the One who was promised. As Andrew approached with Simon, Jesus surveyed him. "Your name is Simon, and your father is called John. But from this day forward you will be known as Peter the Rock."*
  -
- *The next day Jesus travelled to a neighbouring city, Galilee, where He saw a man named Philip. "Come and be my follower," Jesus said, and Phillip could not resist.*
  -
- *Later that day, all excited, Philip ran to find his friend Nathaniel. "Hey, we've found Him! We've found the One we've been waiting for! Jesus, the Anointed One."*
-
- *"Can anything good come out of Nazareth?" Nathaniel retorted.*
-
- *"Come and see for yourself," replied Philip.*

-   When Jesus saw Nathaniel approaching, He said, "Here comes a true citizen—an honest man with no hidden motives."

-   Nathaniel was stunned. "But you've never met me."

-   "Nathaniel, right before Philip came to you I saw you sitting under the shade of a fig tree."

-   Nathaniel broke. "Teacher, you are truly the Son of God. You are the Ruler we have been expecting."

-   Those five went, saw, and became followers of Jesus."

With that, the Fellowship leader issued an invitation.

"Anyone here with us today who would like to meet Jesus? Come and see – your life will never be the same. Give Him a chance today. You must have tried the rest: self-righteousness, free-spiritedness, money, life of luxury, and all such. Now try the best – Jesus! Come and see. Taste and see. Taste the new life of true love, joy, peace and prosperity that only He can give."

Imma's heart was touched by this story, adding to the stirrings from his encounters with the new LuChi and the new Nath. But he had no intention of indicating today that he would go meet Jesus and enter into a personal relationship with Him. *No, thanks!*

He looked over at his friends and was relieved that their eyes were closed. They seemed lost in prayer. Good; no pressures.

The service over, all five got in Imma's car.

"I hope you had a good time?" Tessie asked.

Imma nodded and she chattered on, getting to know him and Gift better.

"Am I the only hungry one here?" asked LuChi. "I don't have any food in my house. Let's stop at a restaurant. Tessie and Gift, you are buying – that's what it will cost you, for now, to join this special trio's gang."

"What else will it cost?" Gift and Tessie asked simultaneously, protesting.

"I will reserve that for later. Imma and Nath know what I'm talking about. But first things first. We are hungry, and buying us food will admit you into our circle – for now." They all laughed.

Dinner over, with Gift and Tessie dropped off at their homes, the gang of three was by themselves. "We have time," said LuChi. "Son of Vine, tell us about Gift. Now that we have seen her, I can't wait to hear all about her. Nath, can you? Wow, she is an angel. Beautiful, truly graceful, and sprightly. And she loves the Lord!"

"I agree. Imma, spill it. What's this *it's complicated*? Your mom didn't hoist someone on you before you met her, did she? And you haven't been sleeping around?"

"No, no, no. Not at all. I may not be like you, dead and all that, but I have my own good values too. It's a long story."

7

Twists and Turns

LuChi and Nath visited Imma together as Nath's furniture was delivered for storage in Imma's home.

"Son of Vine," said LuChi, "Gift's story is item number one on the agenda today. No dodging."

"Agreed," said Nath. "The *complication* will be understood today. And know that God is able to *uncomplicate* things. Come on, man!"

"Spill it all," said LuChi. "We have all day and night. Tomorrow is not a work day."

The two would not be denied. Imma cut to the chase.

Gift's cousin, James, who liked Imma a lot, had introduced them. After a few visits to her home in Lagos, observing her gracefulness, warmth, friendliness and confidence, Imma had become smitten. It didn't take him long to discover that she liked him, too. They became friends, but it was clear that she was holding back. She had shared her faith and invited him to her church a few times, but Imma had rebuffed it all. He didn't think it was a big deal until five months later, when he broached the subject of marriage.

"You know, not long ago I had the good fortune of meeting you, but it's like I've known you all my life. I feel an emptiness on days I don't see or talk to you. I don't know…"

"You don't know what?"

"I don't know the right words. But I like you a lot. I like your company a lot."

"That's interesting. I suppose I guessed that already."

"You guessed?"

"Okay, I know that already." There was a twinkle in her eyes.

"I'm almost done with all the educational programs I want to do for now. I've progressed well in my career. There's just one more box that needs to be checked for me to fully settle down."

"Congrats. Just one? Fortunate you! And that box is?"

"But you know what I mean. Don't you catch my drift?"

"Hmmm, I can guess. But why guess when you are here, and can say what you mean? Not sure I like catching drifts."

"Come on, Gifty! Don't make this hard. I have fallen in love with you."

"That's sweet of you, really appreciated! You must know I like you as well. But love is not a word we use casually."

"I'm not using it casually, Gifty. I really think you are the one I can spend the rest of my life with. The way my heart skips a bit every time I see you…."

"It skips just a bit?" her face turned serious.

"Okay, my heart skips a whole lot every time I see you!"

I was just joking," she laughed. "And you can spend the rest of your life with? Just spend?"

"What do you mean?"

"No qualifiers to spending the rest of your life with someone?"

"Oh, I see what you mean. Okay, I really think you are the one I can happily and peacefully spend the rest of my life with; the one who will complete me."

She laughed again. "That's better."

"You are having fun torturing me!"

"Okay, seriously, I hear you. But Imma, dear, we have a problem."

Demonstrating to his two friends how jolted he was by her we-have-a-problem shot, Imma sank into his chair and leaned forward with a mournful expression on his face. That had brought a quick explanation from Gift.

"I will only tell a man I love him if I have prayed about him and received affirmation that he's *the one*. With you, I can't even get to the stage of praying, because you are different. We are not on the same page in terms of our faith. I am a Believer. Regrettably, you are not – the last time I checked."

"I believe in God."

"I am talking about a personal relationship with God. About faith in Jesus Christ's death and resurrection. That's different. Let me tell you why I would say no – why we have a problem. Jesus has to be in my marriage, in my home. The only way that can happen is if the man I marry shares the same faith in Him.

"Imma, imagine if Jesus was not part of our wedding? I have no illusions – all marriages have challenges. There is no marriage where the initial love, happiness, harmony or commitment does not wane from time to time. There is likely no marriage that will not experience a lack of something. Lack of finances, a job, or a business gone awry. I want Jesus Christ to be part of my marriage so that if – no, not if, but when – such a lack happens He will save the day, as He did in Cana.

"And, lest I forget, I cannot complete you. I don't think any human can complete another. Only God can complete a person – make a person a secure and confident, including as a partner in a marriage."

Imma turned to his friends. "Son of Shepherd, Nath the Bulldozer, there you have it. Gift and I have a problem. It *is* complicated. You understand what I'm saying? She cited the Bible for her insistence on Jesus being in her marriage – the wedding feast where Jesus turned water into wine. Recently, she talked to me about this same personal relationship thing with Jesus and I told her I'd have none of it. I'm good with my religion."

"I can see that it looks complicated," replied Nath. "But to be honest, I don't think it's you and Gift who have a problem. I think it's you that have a problem. Or, to word it better, a challenge."

"I agree with Nath," said LuChi. "In fact, I'll go farther and say it's an opportunity."

"How is it not our problem?" asked Imma. "She says she likes me as well. If she is going to insist on the man she marries being like her, like you, how is that not a problem for her, too? Suppose she doesn't find such a man, and at a time she wants him? Women are on a clock, you know. Well, I'm available now. And that window won't remain open forever."

"Son of Vine, I can see you're upset, but don't talk like that. No window is closing. In fact, what you may have is wider – a door. The question is whether you will do the right thing," LuChi said, grinning.

"Like what?"

"Like seriously consider being on same page with her on this faith matter. You should seriously consider entering into a personal relationship with Jesus."

"And not just because of Gift," Nath jumped in. "It's something we already recommended you do. LuChi and I didn't give our lives to Jesus because we wanted to get married, or to meet any gal's requirement. We did it because we were tired of life as it was. We turned it over to Him. And He has changed our lives – given us love, joy, peace, purpose, destiny. That this now qualifies us to marry someone of the same faith is just a bonus. An expression of His continued goodness. That's all it is. After all, there are people who may never get married – Believers in Jesus or not."

"I agree again," said LuChi. "The issue of faith is not primarily about who you marry. I say primarily, because, marriage is important. I can't lie to you, my brother – I want to get married. After all, God said that it is a mystery, like the relationship between Him and His Church. I'm not sure I understand it all, but if He said so about marriage, there must be something great about it. We are told that when Jesus comes to take His own to Heaven it will be like a wedding feast where He will be the groom and we the resplendent bride clothed in glistening white. Marriage is important. It's in the Bible: 'It's not good for a man to be alone.' And I like the sound of the sweet wine. Man, do I salivate for it, do I want to taste it...drink it. Bring it on, men! I can't wait for that day. The love, the romance, and the consummation. The intimacy. I can't wait, men. I'm not a eunuch."

"Watch your language, man." Nath was uncomfortable with LuChi being that graphic. "Get serious."

"What are you talking? That's a serious matter, man. Are you not looking forward to the night of the wedding day? The honeymoon? Don't be over-spiritual."

"Hey, you guys," Imma said, "I am religious, and I pray too. I love Gift – that should be all that matters."

"Respectfully, Imma, she's the only one who can say what matters for her. You should be glad she told you. The ball is in your court."

Five days after this conversation with Nath and LuChi, Imma started preparing for the long drive to his Umunumo rural town for a vacation. He liked to spend some of his holidays there, to enjoy the quiet and the lush green scenery of the countryside as well as have some quality time with family. With Mama in particular.

The previous night he had gone to see Gifty, getting in some quality time prior to going away for two weeks.

"Thanks for taking me to your friends' Fellowship event," she said. "I liked it a lot. I like LuChi and Nath even more. And Tessie too."

"No surprises there."

Gift smiled broadly, revealing her beautiful white teeth that contrasted with her ebony black complexion. "Yes, no surprises there."

"But I certainly hope you are not as weird. That I am not dealing with a split personality here: dead and alive. And that you have not jettisoned your aspirations for a dream life because of Jesus."

"I have a transformation story as well, if that's what you are asking. I was religious, perhaps like you are now, and living life to the full as I understood it. I liked to party with my friends and family, and I thought all there was to life was to complete my education, get a job, be married and live happily ever after. But then I met a roommate in university who with her kindness and calmness gave me a glimpse of the Jesus life…

"Imma, it's getting late. You have a long drive ahead of you tomorrow. Go home and get some sleep. We can talk about my new aspirations when you get back. Say me well to your family. I'll be praying for you."

A quick hug, and ten minutes later Imma stepped on the gas. He needed to get home, pack and get sufficient sleep for the long trip. But he couldn't get Gift out of his mind. Wasn't she beautiful? Kind, confident, and secure. Graceful. Sprightly. He wished he hadn't planned this trip that was taking him away from her for almost ten days. How could he live the rest of his life without her?

Am I willing to do what they say is necessary to make her part of my life?

That night Imma made his resolve. The problem standing in the way of marrying Gift would be solved, one way or the other.

He woke the next morning with a voice in his head. Unmistakably Mama's. She was a strong woman with strong orthodox religious beliefs. Imma and his siblings had been raised on those beliefs. Conservative and dogmatic, they differed considerably from the new faith to which he had just been exposed.

Would Mama tolerate any talk of Imma embracing this new faith, this born-again Christianity? Some people Imma had met in the big city characterized it as fanaticism. Imma thought so, too. Knowing his mom, he feared she would think worse. She now respected him and accorded him some independence, but faith and marriage were on an exclusive list and Mama would insist that her opinion counted. Imma hated to upset her.

All this was hypothetical. He hadn't made any decisions yet on faith or Gift, so on this trip there was nothing to worry about. But wouldn't this be an opportunity to test the waters? He began to plot his strategy. He decided to throw out some what-if feelers to gauge Mama's reaction.

Pulling out of his driveway much later than his planned 6 am departure, he took a deep breath. Snaking his way through the heavy traffic, with most of the ten million people who called Lagos home already on his route, he battled vehicles in constant competition for space, people jumping in and out of public buses and spilling onto the road, hawkers shouting out their wares and shoving them into vehicles hoping to find a willing buyer. Imma pitied the few traffic police who whistled and shouted to restore some semblance of order.

Imma burned through two hours just getting out of the city and onto the expressway. He was a careful driver, but he was distracted on this trip by not being able to put LuChi, Nath, Tessie and Gift out of his mind. He chewed gum most of the way.

Those changes in his friends. The joy and peace they exuded... the confidence. The security. The patience. The contentment. The fulfillment. The no-complaints attitude. They had died, and now they lived a new life.

What does all that even mean?

His trip today had a natural split to it: three hours from Lagos to Benin, two hours from Benin to Onitsha, one hour from Onitsha to Owerri, and another one hour to Imma's Umunumo home – all things being equal. But all things were not equal. In fact, they hardly ever were. Large stretches of the road were bad, with only one side of the road in use. And the inter-city route through the centre of each city caused traffic snarls that easily ate up an hour or more.

It didn't matter how often Imma made this trip, the hustle and bustle and unique attractions of each city filled his adventure tank. He gazed in wonder at the carvings and artifacts on display in Benin, the long Niger Bridge that ushered you into Onitsha, and the imposing cathedral standing tall like a welcome monument on the approach to Owerri.

Driving for close to eight hours, stopping just once to get lunch and gas, he played music non-stop. But only for companionship. He couldn't say whose song played, or what was being sung. LuChi and Nath had hacked into his mind. That they were happier than him, more at peace, more confident and more excited, he could not deny. They even looked healthier, and appeared more fulfilled. Notwithstanding that they were less successful financially, the peace and excitement in their lives was undeniable. And, Imma finally admitted to himself, it was attractive....

The questions gripping Imma's heart became stronger. The stuff he had committed his life to pursuing – academic and career success, life of luxury, getting married, making family and friends proud – was that not the path to the dream life? Being religious, trying not to do bad things – was that not enough for God? Was it not the right pathway to true and enduring happiness, peace and fulfillment?

He wavered between considering a personal relationship with Jesus, and dismissing it as peer pressure. His friends cared about him, and Imma found it perfectly understandable that they were trying to influence him. He had to admit, though, that they were people of integrity whose new lives had started to become appealing.

Should I give this new life thing a try?

He mustered all his strength to banish that possibility. Night was approaching, but Imma did not plan to reach his town today. The lights glinting from the cathedral announced his arrival at Owerri, the capital city of his home state. The single-lane road turned into a dual-carriage main street with surprisingly well-trimmed trees on both sides and flowers in the divide gleaming under bright street lights. Imma fished out his stopover address. He was looking forward to visiting Johnny Judah, a university friend, before proceeding to Umunumo.

As Imma sighted Johnny's street and searched for the building, his excitement turned to trepidation. Suppose Johnny had changed? Like LuChi and Nath?

Johnny, you better be the friend I knew.

Johnny, five feet nine, chocolate coloured, strongly built and always with a smile, appeared to be his usual self – warm, hospitable and gentle. They chatted excitedly, catching up. At dinner, however, Imma found the prayer over the food a little unusual. Then it was time to retire for the night.

"Do you mind? I like to read the word and pray before going to bed. Want to join me? No pressures."

"Read the word?"

"I mean the Bible."

"Oh, I see. I think I'll pass. Been a long day."

"No worries. I pray you find your room comfortable for a good rest. I agree you must be tired driving that long distance. See you in the morning."

"Good night."

Imma took a shower and jumped into bed. He wished he could call Gifty to let her know he had arrived and find out how she was doing. *It hasn't even been 24 hours yet!* Imma dismissed that thought. Tomorrow Johnny would have to find him a place to call Gifty.

He surveyed the room. Not bad. Imma wasn't surprised. His mind veered to the dinner prayer and the invitation to read the word and pray before bed. *He seems to be doing well. But is he...? This is not happening: has Johnny changed too? Not another one!*

"Good morning! Breakfast is ready."

"Good morning, Johnny! 'Be there in a minute."

Imma looked at the time. It was already 9 am. "Aren't you running late for work? Go on, I'll take care of myself. I'm a big boy."

"Sure you are, but I took today off to make it a long weekend with my friend. It's been a while, and we need to make the best of this visit. Who knows when the next one will be?" Johnny said, laughing.

They rode in Johnny's car to do some shopping, and to show Imma around town. Returning to a relaxed evening, they watched sports on television, made dinner and caught up some more. Imma respected Johnny and liked him a lot. Johnny was gentle, ever-smiling, intelligent and supportive. If Johnny asked him to join him in whatever again before bedtime, with that smile and love, could he say no?

Johnny always means well. Wants the best for me.

Invite Imma he did. Imma didn't say no. No excuses. He hadn't been driving all day. Johnny read from the Bible, they shared a conversation about it, and Johnny prayed. Briefly enough.

The next morning Johnny shared his program for the day.

"Imma, we'll tour the city a little more today, including a stop to show you my office."

"Sounds good."

"We should be back in time for lunch and some rest. Then I have a program at 6 pm. It's a meeting where professionals go to share their faith journeys and experiences, and those seeking to know more about the faith are welcome. It's organized by a global group called the Full Gospel Businessmen's Fellowship International. It is held at a very nice hotel. Want to come? You'll like it, and you are likely to meet people you know – old friends and school mates. It is popular with professionals and business people, young and old, female and male."

"Sounds like a plan. It's been a while since I spent time in Owerri, and it would be great to meet some old friends. And you say it is a business meeting? So perhaps there's also opportunity to make some business contacts? As you know, we bankers are always looking for opportunities to connect to the business world."

"Yeah, to get some money off them!"

"No; more like to help them with financing and advice for their growth and profitability. And sure, we get opportunities to earn handsomely doing that. Can't deny it."

"It's certainly a good place to connect and start new relationships while building up faith. The potential is great."

8

A Cloud of Dust

The next day, Sunday, his Nissan Bluebird sedan roared into life at the first turn of the ignition. Relief all over his face, Imma was thankful that the battery had survived two days of idleness. The city centre was behind him in fifteen minutes, and he sped up on the highway to his village. Recalling the events of last night at the Full Gospel Businessmen's Fellowship meeting, joy bubbled up from inside, and a peace he had never known enveloped him.

The welcome had struck Imma first. The *Happiest People on Earth*, proclaimed in colourful letters on a stand by the door and on banners hanging on walls across the room. "What a claim," Imma had muttered.

Then his recent struggles with fatigue, anxiety and general discontent came into his mind. He tried to compare that image with what a happy Imma would look like. A happy Imma – something he had recently discovered he most desired. Become like LuChi and Nath – full of life and energy, excited, content, at peace, fulfilled.

Is this meeting making a promise to transform me into one of the Happiest People on Earth?

Imma stood, mouth agape, peering at the head table, confirming that the familiar face he saw was Chris David. Chris was one of the most educated, prominent and respected men from Imma's town, and a top official in their state government. What was he doing here?

Johnny explained that Chris had entered into a personal relationship with Jesus a few years back, and was now an active Believer. Imma caught his breath. At the meeting a medical doctor, an engineer, a police commissioner, a well-known businessman, a university professor, another top government official and a banker all shared testimonies of their personal encounters with Jesus Christ and how He had made their lives more prosperous in various ways. The cream of society. As Imma listened in awe, he recalled LuChi's quip that wise men still seek Jesus.

One of the leaders shared a message from the Bible, then issued an invitation to come meet Jesus and enter into a personal relationship with Him. No pressure, no nudging from Johnny or any of the other friends Imma met there. He stepped out all on his own.

And did it.

"You are now united with Jesus Christ," the preacher declared. "You have become a new person. Your old life is gone, and a new life has begun. This new life is a love gift from our Creator, who has pursued you and brought you into a relationship with Him through the Anointed One, Jesus. He lives in you now by the Holy Spirit. Praise the Lord! Congratulations!"

Imma received a small booklet, *The way of Life in Christ,* to read at home. It would help him gain a better understanding of what had just happened. It would help him learn how to walk and grow in this new life.

Noticing a familiar traffic circle, Imma realized he was only fifteen minutes away from home. For over an hour he had been on overdrive, enraptured in his thoughts and hardly noticing anything.

Until now. As he exited the highway onto the unpaved road that meandered through farms to his family home, a canopy of palm, coconut, pea and orange trees in full bloom came into beautiful view. Birds flew from tree to tree, floating individually or in picturesque formations, producing beautiful music as they chirped away. Mother hens with their chicks in tow, goats and sheep criss-crossed the road and between the farmlands with no care in the world for the danger posed by Imma's car. In the countryside there was a great harmonic co-existence of humans, animals and birds that was absent in the cities. Imma smiled, saluting their right to share the road. He slowed and gently tooted the horn to shoo them out of the way, exercising his own rights.

The lush crops and vegetation of the farms flooded Imma with memories of farming, stirring up deep emotions. Farming had exposed his greatest weakness and vulnerability in life, but Imma was happy that it also drove his resolve to be a good student. He mused on how his hatred of farming led to the love of education and the great escape. In a strange way, he owed whatever progress he had made in the pursuit of the dream life to his interesting relationship with farming.

He came to his senses. *Mama*! Knowing the tough talk to come dissolved any hope of a pleasant holiday in the village. Approaching the house, he sounded the horn and someone opened the gate. Mama stood by the front door, in spotted yellow *ankara* wrapper and blouse and silk scarf, beaming, as Imma drove in. Fair-skinned with dark hair and almost six feet tall, those smiles still lit up her face and made her even more beautiful. At over sixty years of age, the toil of farming, trading and raising nine children with limited resources have begun to show. Imma saw the wrinkles. Her recent poorly health still failed to diminish her beauty and dignity. A more-than-conqueror, that one!

If only she knew who just drove in. When she finds out, will she still be smiling?

That thought gave him the shivers. The Imma she had bidden goodbye to the last time he visited, the Imma she had got messages from right up to last week, had died...

On the second evening of his visit, as he walked back home from checking on extended family and friends around the village, Imma savoured the fresh air. Replete with all the refreshments they had provided and lugging the bags of take-away fruits they gave him, Imma looked forward to an early night. A heavy rain the previous evening had washed off the dust and dryness; Imma would exchange this soft, cool breeze any day for the fans and air conditioners of the city. But his dream of a restful sleep vanished when Mama requested a chat after dinner.

Imma dreaded *the talk*. So far he had chatted with Papa and Mama informally, generally about their health and how things were at home. But those talks were nothing like the chat Mama had just scheduled. Imma scratched at his dinner. He braced himself.

Seize the moment. After Mama tables her agenda I'll share mine. We'll get it all done with!

Dinner over, Imma's mom joined him in his room. At times like this he appreciated his dad all the more. His dad hardly had any concerns, and was as informal as they came.

Mama ran down her list, and when she announced that she was done Imma heaved a sigh of relief. Nothing new; no relationship strainers. He could handle the lecture on financial prudence. Imma thanked her and re-assured her that he was mindful of his responsibilities and doing his best to meet her expectations.

As Mama spoke traditional blessings over him and made to leave, Imma struck.

"Mama, I have heard you. I also want to tell you something special."

"What my son? Go ahead."

"I made a decision three days ago to take my relationship with God to another, personal level."

"What does that mean?"

"I made Jesus Christ my personal Saviour and Lord"

"I don't understand. You have always been religious."

"Yes, but this is not religion. This is about a personal relationship with Jesus Christ. It is different, Mama."

"Is this about those groups of people who say they are born again? Those fanatics? Where their leaders ask them to give all their money to God, all the while enriching themselves? No way, my son! They will make you abandon me and your family!"

"No such thing, Mama. How could I ever abandon you and my family? If anything, I will love and care for you more with the love of Jesus that is now pouring out of my heart."

"One more important thing I wanted to tell you. On this marriage thing you have been hounding me with, I want you to know that I haven't forgotten. In fact, there's a young woman I like so much. I am still praying about it, though. And she has to pray about it, too, to be sure…"

"Pray? Is she one of those born-again people too?"

"Yes, Mama."

"So she is the one who enticed you into this fanatic group? And wants to steal you from us?"

"It's not like that, Mama."

"How is it then? These nice young women here that your dad and I have been telling you about – none of them is good enough for you? You want to ignore them because you saw a big-city girl who is born again? I had my fears about your going to Lagos!"

Mama stormed out. Imma's attempt to calm her and reassure her had failed.

Three days before the end of Imma's vacation, a knock on his door came as the second cockcrow sounded. Instinctively Imma closed his eyes tighter, pretending he was still asleep, until he heard a respectful greeting from his mom and a polite enquiry as to whether the time was convenient for him to chat.

Imma heaved a sigh of relief: this wasn't a wake-up knock to go work on the farm! It had been more than two decades since he had been delivered from forced farm work, but roosters crowing still did him in. He muttered a quick thank you to whoever had invented education and occupation such as banking, then dressed and opened the door for Mama.

"My son, you know that the traditional age grade initiation festival is coming up early next year. We have started preparing here for that. And I hope you are, too."

"Mama, with my new faith I can no longer join in any event that does not glorify God. All such traditional and religious things are no longer for me."

"I see. So our culture and traditions are no longer good enough for you? You are now superior to them and all of us? If your plan is to embarrass the family and cause my early death, you will succeed!"

She slammed the door behind her.

Imma's dad came out. "What's going on?"

"Just a misunderstanding with Mama."

"About what?"

"I shared my decision to grow in my spiritual life and she doesn't seem to like that."

"Strengthening your relationship with God is not a bad thing. Why would she not like that?"

"I've also found a girl I think I would like to marry and she's pushing back."

"I don't understand – she's been clamouring for you to get married. What's wrong with the girl?"

"Nothing. Mama thinks I got born-again because of her."

"My son, I'll speak with your mother. I've always trusted your judgment and know you will do the right thing. But be sensitive to your mother's feelings. And this girl, when will we meet her?"

"I haven't even proposed to her yet. Depending on how things go, maybe when we come home for Christmas."

Imma appreciated God for his dad!

Going back to his room, Imma assessed the situation and came to the conclusion that it was best for everyone if he took himself out of the now-toxic and deteriorating environment. As he got ready he counted out the upkeep money to leave with them, his mom getting the biggest share as usual. Just then, she called him to breakfast.

"I'm not hungry, Mama. I need to get going so I arrive before nightfall."

"Get going where?"

"To Lagos."

"Didn't you say you were resuming work next week? That's five days from now. And that you would be here till the weekend?"

"Yes, Mama, but I need to do some personal errands in Lagos before I resume. Once I go back to work I hardly have any time for such. Also, I need time to recover from the long trip. I will write often, and come home again soon to see you."

Though upset with Mama, he didn't want to leave her in a sad state, particularly given her recent poor health. That was a major concern to Imma. He went to her room where she had retreated, but she lay on the bed and looked away. Mama was too strong to cry. Some had nicknamed her *ears,* lion, both for her strong will and industry. So, no surprise at her dry eyes. And she responded to nothing Imma said, except when he pulled out the wad of money and held it out to her. She reached out and took it.

"I thought you would refuse the money!" Imma tried a joke, laughing.

Her eyes still avoided his, and she would not flatter him with a reaction. Money had kept its distance from Mama's life. Lack of money had torpedoed or delayed many of her dreams. She would not steal, but any time legitimate money came near she seized it.

Mama's countenance sent an unequivocal message to Imma that she didn't agree with his new life, or his abrupt departure. She would not come out of her room. Going back to his own room, Imma weighed the matter again and came to terms with it. For the first time in forever, his mom might not be standing at the gate waving until Imma was out of view. That would break his heart. And hers. 'I can't live with that,' Imma muttered, sighing.

He went back to her room.
"Mama, please I need you to release me to go. I'm sorry again that I'm cutting short my visit. But promise I'll come again as soon as I can."

"When?"

"It's just a few months to Christmas. I'll surely be here then. But I'll be sending messages and gifts before that time."

"The age grade initiation is more important to me. I can't bear to have you…"

"Okay Mama. Allow me time to pray about it and consider if and how I can participate."

"Safe journey." She turned and faced the wall.

With his bags and gifts for LuChi and Nath – supplied by their parents - loaded in the trunk, Imma backed out of the gate of his village home. Under different circumstances his rear view mirror would show Mama standing and waving as he drove out of the driveway. Today there was only a cloud of dust. His pulse pounding in his arteries, he headed for Lagos a few days early.

9

Bumps in the Road

Encouraged by the conveners, Imma had bought some resources at the meeting Johnny had taken him to. *That meeting.* The resources included a Bible – what Johnny called the *Good Book* – as well as message and song CDs. "You now have a new kind of life. You will be hungry, you will be thirsty, and will need to feed yourself with a new kind of food. You are like a newborn baby who needs plenty of milk. That food, that milk, is the Word of God," they counselled. Lovingly. Caringly.

Imma slotted one of the CDs into his car stereo. *Not sure whether this is hunger or thirst, but I need to occupy my mind with something right now.* The message began to play. He battled to focus as his mind wandered back over the events of the past few days, including the fallout with his mom. Imma paid attention when he heard, "Let me tell you a story." He rewound the CD a little.

"I want to say a few words regarding the relationship of the Believer and society. It needs to be one of love – God's kind of love: compassion, kindness, gentleness, respect and honour. These don't mean the absence of conflict or disagreement. So don't kid yourself that there will always be agreement between you and those who don't yet share our faith in Jesus Christ. We can disagree respectfully. But we must not compromise our faith in the name of tolerance, accommodation, love or honour. We must gently, graciously, firmly remain committed to Jesus and our faith. Jesus calls us to radical commitment. Yes, even when it threatens relationships in our own family. You've heard that God said we should honour our parents, and we must. But that honour does not include compromising or denying our faith.

"Let me tell you a story of the kind of radical commitment the Christian life calls for. One day Jesus gathered and taught His followers: 'Perhaps you think I've come to spread peace and calm over the earth? I tell you my coming will bring conflict and division. Yes, don't ever think that I have come to make life cozy. No. I came with a sword to cut between son and father, daughter and mother, wife and mother-in-law. To cut through any encumbering cozy relationships and free you for God. Well-meaning family members can be your worst enemies! If you prefer father or mother over Me, you don't deserve Me. If you love son or daughter more than Me, you are not worthy of Me. If you don't take up your cross and follow Me, that is, go all the way with Me, through thick and thin, you are not fit to be My disciple. To find your life, you must lose your life. And whoever loses his life for My sake will find it. I repeat: only those who let go of their lives for My sake and surrender it all to Me will discover true life.'"

Don't ever think that I have come to make life cozy. How did this guy know?

The message continued. "Jesus also made it clear: 'And everything I've taught you is so that the peace which is in me will be in you, and will give you great confidence as you rest in me. In this world you will have troubles, resistance and opposition. But be courageous and of good cheer because I have overcome on your behalf.'"

That was reassuring. But how would He do it? Help Imma in his current trouble?

"I guess I have a lot to learn," Imma said, encouraging himself.

Again breaking just once for lunch and gas, Imma continued on the nine-hour drive to Lagos. Between the messages on the CDs, he reflected on what had transpired on this trip.

I've never felt so much joy! So much peace! But when have I left home without a big goodbye hug from Mama? The first time in forever.

As he carried the last piece of luggage into his house, Imma picked up his mail. Flipping through, he saw a greeting card in a pink envelope. He recognized the handwriting and tore it open.

Since there is no telephone in your remote village and I'm not likely to hear from you till you return, I wanted to be the first to say welcome back to Lagos. Still praying for you.

Your friend, Gift

PS: Don't kid yourself, I didn't miss you too much.

Oh Gifty! Imma read it over and over, savouring the sweetness.

He hadn't forgotten about Gift on his trip. He had been able to call her just once, from Johnny's office. It was impossible to call from his rural town or to send a card. And he was not sure that he would have been inclined to contact her from the village after the encounter with his mom.

Should I go see Gifty? She isn't expecting me. It's still two days before my original return date. I need the time. Maybe I will surprise her tomorrow. How do I break the news? How will it make her feel? LuChi and Nath, too?

Bedtime came. Imma picked up the Bible, read a passage from the Gospel of John, and had a *conversation with God.* Wasn't that how Johnny had described it? "The Bible is God's love letter to His children, and we read it to enjoy that love and reflect on His thoughts and ways. Prayer is to hold a conversation with God, and bedtime prayer is to thank Him, share our day's highs and lows, listen with our heart to His response, ask Him any questions, and make any requests."

He read Gift's card again, and was still clutching it to his heart when he succumbed to sleep.

At 4 pm the next day Imma was at Gift's office, targeting her closing time. He waited patiently in the lobby. When she still hadn't shown up by 4:30 pm, Imma wondered if he had miscalculated. Suppose she wasn't at work, or was working at another branch of her bank? He refrained from asking the receptionist to call her, so as not to spoil the surprise.

Exercise some faith. You are now a man of faith, remember?

At 5 pm on the dot, more people emerged from the elevator. The sprightly steps were ever so fast, but just before she made it to the door, Imma spoke from behind her.

"Aren't you forgetting to receive your visitor, young lady?"

"Imma! What are you doing here?"

Embrace.

"Surprise! To see you and give you a ride home."

"What's today's date? You are not supposed to be back until tomorrow night. Did you run out of money?" She laughed. "Did you miss Lagos too much?"

"No on both counts. How about 'did I miss *somebody* too much?"

"Well, did you miss *somebody* too much? That *somebody* wouldn't be me. Otherwise, I would have known."

"How would you have known?"

"A second call, a card, some message or something. In almost two weeks."

"I thought you people knew things by the Spirit? That God tells you things directly? I relied on Him making my presence known to you. He must have. Your fault, not mine," Imma said, laughing out loud. "Anyway, I am here now."

"Yes, you are. So nice and thoughtful of you to pay me this surprise visit in the office!" She gave Imma another hug. "Let's get out of here before the traffic gets any worse. Where did you park? I can't wait to hear all about your trip!"

All? Don't think so. At least not yet.

Surprisingly, traffic was light, and in less than 30 minutes Imma and Gift were at her home.

Dinner was already made.

"You must be hungry. Or did your mom feed you enough to last a few more days?"

"Quite the contrary. She didn't get that opportunity."

"What do you mean? You were home but not home? Gallivanting with those village friends?"

"No, no. Some days I was too happy to eat. On others I *fasted.* Or let's just say I didn't have an appetite and went without."

"Don't believe you! Fasted*?* What do you know about fasting*!* Meaningful fasting is done by those who have made Jesus their Lord and Saviour. All others just do a hunger strike or weight loss and call it fasting. There's no fasting without reading the Word and praying. The last time I checked, those were not in your profile."

Gift's sister Sharon came down from upstairs.

"Before you both finish my food, note that my husband hasn't eaten! I did not make provision for an additional person, least of all a man who has been on a hunger strike, or fasting, or whatever."

Would make a great sister-in-law.

"Don't mind her," said Gift. The food will be more than enough for five more people. How hungry are you, Imma?"

"Whatever quantity you are eating, I'll have double."

"Welcome, Imma," said Sharon. "Trust you had a good trip."

"I did, thanks. And thanks for being proactive on the food. How did you know I was coming? You will make a great mother-in-law!"

"How about sister-in-law? That will come first."

They all laughed.

Imma and Gift took a short walk in the neighbourhood. He told her more about his trip, and in turn he caught up on her news. Public power had just failed, but they managed to hold a decent conversation despite the deafening noise of the private generators. One mark of the middle class in Lagos was ownership of private generators. The public electricity supply was so erratic that the National Electric Power Authority's acronym, NEPA, was read in derision by the populace as 'never expect power always'. They joked that the utility's only success was in enriching importers of generators, making the ability to self-provide power for one's home a status symbol.

Imma could not resist the aroma of *suya*, the local beef delicacy barbecued openly in the kiosks that dotted the streets outside the gates of most of these middle-class homes. He always admired the security guards and gatemen for their ingenuity in using *suya* and convenience store businesses to occupy their downtime and supplement their meagre income. Giving Gift a lecture on supporting the less privileged, they patronized a *suya* man and treated themselves as they strolled.

"Seriously, what was that about being too happy to eat, fasting and not having appetite? Everything okay?"

"Everything is okay. In fact, I can say this was the best trip I ever went on."

"Really? I'm happy for you then."

Imma was still not ready to tell her that he had entered into a personal relationship with Jesus and become a Believer. Like her. Like LuChi and Nath. He wanted to make sure he could share it in such a way he wouldn't be misunderstood. The struggle continued in his mind. *I like Gifty. I fell in love with her, and would like to spend the rest of my life with her. If confirmed by God in prayer, they had said. But I made Jesus my Saviour and Lord for me, above all.*

"Imma, I would like to hang out longer with you and finish catching up, but it's getting late. Safety first! And sorry, my sister may have had extra food for you, but there's no extra room. Go home!"

"Are you sure on the extra room?" They both laughed. "I agree. And you must also be tired after your long day at the office. Go get some rest and sleep. We'll see each other in a few days."

"A few days?"

"Two days. I have errands to run tomorrow, and then back to the office the day after. But I will call you. And thanks for the card. Very thoughtful of you. The best welcome I've ever had! Read it several times. The words on the card – it was like you were right there talking to me."

"Wondered if you had checked your mail yet."

"First thing. And yours was the first I opened. In fact, the only one I opened the night I got back. Was like cold water to a weary soul."

Gift stopped, with eyes wide open and hand on Imma's shoulder. "Where did you learn that? 'As cold waters to a thirsty soul, so is good news from a far country' is in the Bible. You didn't start reading the Bible in your village, did you?"

"Gifty, I've told you I'm not an infidel. But I wasn't quoting the Bible; just expressed how your sweet card made me feel. But who knows, your Holy Spirit may have given me that expression for you," Imma teased.

"Anyway, you're welcome. Don't get any run-away ideas though. Just being a good friend."

"I know. I read the part about not kidding myself. And I didn't forget about *the problem*."

"Good."

Imma walked her back to the gate of her home and gave her a gentle good-night hug. Driving home, Imma was excited. First, he congratulated himself. He hadn't said it, hadn't told her he was born again. At least he hadn't said it out loud. But he had dodged a bullet with the Bible passage. Mere coincidence. He was glad he hadn't bitten at the opportunity. Imma was genuinely appreciative of her card, especially knowing she made sure he would see it first thing on his return. Her genuine excitement at his surprise visit, her sister's friendliness, the nice walk and chat, and she wanting to see him again soon - *are those messages*?

Imma was smitten all over again.

Problem is gone. But I haven't prayed yet. She hasn't prayed yet. What if God says no?

"Imma, don't get ahead of yourself," he said out loud.

10

Mountains and Valleys

Imma arranged to meet LuChi and Nath at Nath's home. He couldn't wait to share his testimony. And, well, his 'testing'. *Now I get it: that encounter with Mama was the first test of my faith!*

LuChi had arrived at Nath's home before Imma, and was first to the door. "Son of Vine, welcome back! How was everybody at home? Your family, Nath's family and mine? Don't dare tell me that you didn't have time to skip over to our homes to check on our families. You know that won't be acceptable."

"Son of Shepherd, good to see you man! Glad to be back. And what do you mean check on your families? Did you provide me any money for the extra petrol to drive to your homes?"

"Imma, welcome! LuChi, why ask the obvious? I'm going straight to his car trunk to fish out the goodies our mothers sent us. I don't have time for arguments about petrol or engine oil money. Did Imma suddenly become poor? If the trunk is empty, I'll have to be restrained from bulldozing something or somebody."

"Don't mind him. He doesn't need to drive to get to our homes. Thank God for academics, otherwise some people will starve from physical laziness!"

Imma sat down and pleaded his innocence.

"I'm not lazy; just not cut out for farming."

LuChi peered at him, shaking his head.

"So those of us who farmed and those that still do were born with farming DNA and you were not?"

"Son of his father, don't change history. Your mom has told us the story of your farm-dodging stunts - feigned headaches, stomach aches, anything that attracted sympathy. She said when those didn't work, you plead for the option to fetch water from the stream while the others toiled in the soil."

LuChi came over to Imma and tapped him on the shoulder. "That was creative, but laziness nonetheless," he said, laughing.

"Call it what you may. Man, those people were brutal – my mom in particular. My dad was the gentle, happy, easy-to-please parent. My mom? The opposite. Her expectations and demands must be met. Falling short was attributed to laziness and met with consequences. Farming days were the worst in my life! "

"It wasn't that bad. I actually enjoyed going to the farm." LuChi said

"Did they wake you up at unholy hours and force you to the farm? I don't know what part my mom told you, Nath, and you can't judge from hearing one side."
"What else is there to hear beyond your failed scheming?" LuChi asked.

Imma shifted in his chair and took a sip of his *coca cola*

"I'll lay it out for you. From age five growing up, I remember the first cock crow piercing the quiet of the village about 4 am. That announcement of dawn only made me turn and slide deeper into sleep. When more roosters joined the chorus at 6 am, everybody else got up. No one could ignore the chirping of birds in the trees all around the family compound, those rough whisky-laden voices of scolding crows, and the fluttering of feathers as the roosters came down from their own beds to begin the day. Except me. I would close my eyes tighter, praying that I would not be shaken from bed. But it was always futile. Kicking and crying, they dragged me out and gave me cold water to wash my face – to make me clear-eyed to confront the reality of duty. Did any of you face such child abuse?"

"Nath grew up in the city, Enugu, and wouldn't know what you're talking about. But I must confess, I wasn't denied sleep that early to go to the farm."

"Oh, how much I wanted to escape that hard life of machetes, hoes, and blistered hands! Over time it became a constant source of friction, often earning Mama's discipline. "No farming? No eating."

Nath became sympathetic. "Your mom didn't tell me this part. I can understand why you hate farming. How about your siblings?"

"That's what made it worse for me. They all embraced it and some even excelled at it. That perplexed and irritated me, as I stuck out like a sore thumb. Over time it became a constant source of friction, often earning me Mama's discipline. "No farming? No eating."

Imma got up and announced, "Your parents gave some farm produce for you. Let's go get them. I'll tell you the rest of my farming odyssey on the way."

As they walked to his car parked on the street a few meters from Nath's apartment, Imma continued.

"Everybody in my village was forced to farm – whether you were in school or working in some other job. If you lived there, you farmed. LuChi, it must be same in your village right? Though you stayed at your dad's teaching stations sometimes, you should have noticed?

"At 7 am the village families all trooped out of their homes, an all-hands-on-deck labour force filing across the town and into the tiny fields scattered around the village. With baskets of hoes, machetes, seedlings and water hoisted on their heads, I and my siblings would join in the trudge to the fields. Though I hated the early morning wake-up, I agreed that starting early limited the time we laboured in the full blast of the tropical heat."

LuChi concurred. "Oh yeah, everybody farmed in my village too. It was a hard life without modern farming implements. But how else would they have survived?"

"Good point. We depended on the yam, cocoyam, cassava and vegetables scraped from the farms to feed the many mouths in each family. And I joined in the prayer that there would be some produce left over to sell for supplemental income – to pay school fees and the like."

"School was your escape, then. You should thank God that farming helped to pay for your education," Nath said, pointing to the bright side.

"Even in those farming days I enjoyed school! I can still see me holding my dad's hand as walked to the school where he taught. On those trips, Papa would sing songs about alphabets and numbers. Back at home, I would mimic him, sharing what I had learned. On school days I woke up on my own with the second rooster crow, smiling broadly and eager to get going. In school they said mind was a sponge, and I did well academically. My first toys that I proudly displayed to my friends were gifts from Mama and Papa to celebrating my school performance."

LuChi agreed. "You must have been an early bloomer."

"Fortunately so. Mama warned me that doing well in school would not exempt me from farming, but I recognized early that education was a path out of the misery of that farming life. Many years later, I have not fully realized my dreams away from farming. But surely, they don't seem so far away anymore."

"May all our good dreams come true," Nath said, as they got to the car.

"So, I did go see your folks. And they continue to spoil you. This extra load must have cost me extra gas. If I had not changed, I would be asking for a refund."

"You have changed?" LuChi asked.

"Stop fooling around, you two. Open the trunk. In fact, if you want to have dinner on me tonight, whatever Imma brought is what we get to eat. God is good. *Jehovah Jireh!* My Provider! And God bless all moms! How did my mom know that I'm almost out?"

Fifteen minutes later and Nath's yam, cocoa yam, *garri, japummiri* (steamed cassava chips), *ukwa* (oil bean), assorted fruit and palm oil unloaded in the kitchen, LuChi hollered.

"Son of Vine. Come on, spill it! All of it. How was your trip otherwise?"

"Eventful. The good and the not-so-good. Where do you want me to start?"

"The good, of course. Perhaps the good will be so good that we won't care or have time to hear the not-so-good."

Imma went straight to the point.

"Son of Shepherd, Nath the Bulldozer, I gave my life to Jesus. I asked Him into my heart to be my Saviour and Lord. I'm so happy…"

His voice broke. *Joy unspeakable.*

Transfixed momentarily, his two friends stared at him, whispering in unison.

"Say that again – you did what?"

"I gave my life to Christ. I am a Believer in Him. I'm a new man."

They both stood up with unblinking eyes burning, staring. Then they almost pushed him to the ground as they hugged and cried and laughed together. "Praise the Lord! God is good! We knew He would do it."

Nath got up and raised his hands, waving.

"Yes, He is a prayer-answering God. Would He leave our friend unsaved? No way!"

LuChi announced, "This calls for a celebration, man. Big one. We should hold a party, but for tonight let's go to a restaurant and celebrate."

Nath agreed. "Yes, yes, yes! Celebrate we shall. Heaven must have been celebrating since the moment you said yes to Jesus. It's never too late to join that party; we are joining tonight."

"Exactly. The celebration tonight is on me. This reminds me of the homecoming of that guy in the prodigal son story. Son of Vine, I don't know if you felt like the prodigal son or not, and I'm not as rich as his father, but I feel like throwing a party. Welcome home, bro, this is where you belong."

"Very apt, LuChi, let's throw a prodigal-son welcome-home party tonight. Let's start with some drinks here. We can go out later if need be."

Imma knew his friends would be excited, but nothing to this extent. He raised his hand to get in a word.

"What's prodigal-son style?"

Nath had started bringing out juice drink, biscuits and meat. So Imma looked to LuChi.

"You must know that popular Bible story? I forgot, you are too green and haven't read the Bible enough." LuChi laughed his heart out.

Nath took over.

"This our Jesus. Love Him! Awesome communicator. Told all kinds of beautiful stories – some called them parables – to drive home the most complex truth and lessons. The prodigal son story was one of three stories He told to give us a glimpse of what happens in Heaven when one yet-to-be-Believer meets Him and invites Him into his or her life. Let me start with the learning He communicated through those three stories:

There's more joy in Heaven over one sinner's rescued life than there is over ninety-nine good people in no need of rescue.

God's angels throw a party in Heaven every time one lost soul turns to God; every time a sinner's heart changes to knowing that 'God is for me, not against me.'

"Now the prodigal son story itself:

The younger of a wealthy man's two sons asked for his portion of his inheritance, and went away to have a good life. Unfortunately for him, a famine occurred after he had squandered it all on easy living. He couldn't get a job to take care of himself. Tail between his legs, he came home, fell on his dad's shoulders seeking forgiveness and willing to be one of his dad's servants, no longer a son. The father wasn't even listening to him. Still locked in the embrace of his son, he called out to the servants. "Quick, bring a clean set of clothes and dress him. Put the family ring on his finger and sandals on his feet. Roast the fattened cow! We're going to feast! We're going to celebrate! My son is here! He was dead, and is now alive! Given up for lost, and now found!" And what celebration and rejoicing they had!

"So, there you go, son of his father. We are joining Heaven in that celebration!"

The appetizers over, they started off for the restaurant as LuChi had insisted. Moreover, he was still hungry. As usual.

"We haven't even asked: son of Vine, how did this transformation happen?"

Imma told them all about the meeting Johnny had taken him to at the hotel.

"To be clear, this wasn't about Gift. Since my reunion with you guys, starting with that first night LuChi visited me, I have been re-examining my life. So this was about what had been stirring in my heart, and about my search for fulfillment. I could not deny that I needed more than material success to achieve the abundant life of contentment. That day at the Full Gospel Businessmen's Fellowship meeting in Owerri I saw our town's other *Big Boy*, Chris David, and other successful professionals. That allayed one of the concerns I had – that this new life of personal faith in Jesus Christ would jeopardize my aspiration to be successful. I saw people who were successful and still exuded joy, peace, contentment, and fulfillment. I could no longer restrain myself from accepting the invitation to make Jesus my Saviour and Lord. And to enjoy what you both and Gift have."

Sensing their eagerness to hear more, Imma continued. "I am grateful for the love of you four – Gift, Johnny, and both of you – in bearing witness through your lives and words to the love, peace, joy, fulfillment and contentment that come from having a personal relationship with Jesus Christ. But I did this for me."

"Right on, man! We each did it for ourselves, too."

"But I can't help wondering what Gift will think. That I'm just doing this to get her to marry me? I would hate to think..."

"Son of Vine, stop right there! She won't think any such thing. We now know her. She's not one to attribute your conversion to herself. She knows full well that only God can convert a person. Lots of other people were praying for you to see the need for a personal relation with Jesus. Including our new friends from our Fellowship, Amara and her sister, Onyinye."

"By the way, thanks for helping Amara get a placement in your bank for her internship."

"She got accepted?"

"Yeah, got the offer last week and she's been over the moon. She couldn't contact you in your remote village to convey her gratitude. You should see her next week when she starts."

"And yes, Amara has also been praying for you to be saved. Is somebody going to say you were saved so you can marry her, too? Or so she can marry you? Don't waste your time on such thoughts. Even if people think or say things, just ignore them."

"Glad she got the placement. And yeah, I've come to appreciate her and her sister a lot. Such strong characters. I'm indebted to them, you, Gifty and all who were genuinely interested in my well-being, in my soul. When my story is written, you will all get a prominent place," Imma said, smiling.

LuChi, Nath and Imma were still excited, but concerned with Imma's worry about Gift.

"I can't see Gift wanting to take credit for what only God can do. I'm not telling any more stories today, but doesn't the *Good Book* say no one can come to Jesus except the Father draws him or her?"

"It says that?"

"Oh, you haven't reached there yet?" LuChi liked to tease. "You are still green. I will give you the reference to go read for yourself. People can connect and introduce others to Jesus, but only God can convert. And the passage is in the Gospel of John."

"Gospel of John? That's where they asked me to start my daily reading. It's still baby steps for me."

"It's in John 6:44 to be exact. You will get there, don't worry."

"And you know that by heart?"

Nath smiled. "When you make God's Word your daily bread – reading, studying and meditating – some will surely stick in your heart and in your mouth."

LuChi steered the conversation back to Gift.

"You said you saw Gift the day after you got back. What did she say?"

"I didn't tell her. I haven't told her."

"What? I don't want to be there when she finds out you have kept this testimony from her all these days!"

"I told you, I didn't want her thinking that... I was concerned."

"You are mistaken. She would have celebrated like we did, giving all the glory to God. She would not dare want to share the glory with Him. All the glory goes to God. Always. Anyone who has been a Believer knows that. Gift certainly knows that. We just introduce Jesus to people; only God converts. And who says you will get married? She still has to pray, and you still have to pray. What if God says you're not the best fit for each other? That there's a better, sweeter fit for you? And for her?"

"Okay, I'll tell her tomorrow."

"And recall that in two days she has invited us to her own Fellowship event? Should be a great time. And Nath's new *belle* is coming too. Right? Can't wait to meet her!"

"Yes. Dorcas will be there."

"And Tessie of course. Let's all meet there. Won't be fair to ask Son of Vine to run round the whole city picking every one. Moreover, his car is only a five-seater."

"And a reminder: please give Gift the good news before we all meet up. Like I said, I don't want to be there…"

"Don't worry, Son of Vine. I'll pray that Gift understands and spares you."

The next day, Imma left early from work to pick up Gift at her office. It was supposed to be a short drive, but on a Friday afternoon he was able to weave only slowly through the traffic. *I can't go beyond the speed limit. I'm a new man.* He was constantly reminding himself of that these days. New life, new behaviour, new fruits, as they said at most of the Fellowship meetings he had attended so far.

His dashboard clock read 3:50 pm as he parked opposite Gift's office. *Thank God. I'd hate to keep her waiting.* Gift was a stickler for time, and they had agreed on 4 pm. Imma sighted her crossing with her hair swaying gracefully in the light wind, and waved. Otherwise, finding him in that overfilled parking lot would be like looking for a needle in a haystack.

"Hey, best friend. Over here!"

Her face broke into a broad smile. He hugged her, appreciating her more and relishing her thoughtful card. Driving her home, they chatted about their day. Imma put on the car stereo, turning up the volume a little. He had purposely chosen a CD from the resources bought at Johnny's meeting. He set it to a particular song, one that had ministered so much to him and that captured what had happened to him... what he wanted to convey to Gift.

> *He touched my life with His hands, my life changed*
> *He touched my life with His hands, my life changed*
> *He touched my heart with His hands*
> *I became a brand new man*
> *Jesus touched my life with His hands, my life changed*

"Nice song. Your friend Johnny gave you that? I'm surprised."

"Gifty, there's something I want to tell you."

"What? Go on, tell me!"

"I asked Jesus into my life." Imma broke into a broad smile. "I made Him my Saviour and my Lord! I am a brand new man."

"What? You?"

"Yes I did! I'm so happy! I've never known this kind of peace! It's wonderful! Johnny invited me to a Full Gospel Businessmen's Fellowship on the third night of my trip, and it happened!" He was tearing up.

Gift unbuckled her seat belt, leaned over and enfolded him in a big embrace.

"Oh my God! Praise the Lord! Wonderful!"

The car swerved and she quickly let go, suddenly realizing he was driving.

"Thank you! Yes, praise the Lord! He has given me a new life. He has changed me."

Imma waited for more reaction, but she shifted as far away from him as she could and curled up by the window, quiet. The smile on her face vanished. He remembered Nath's prophecy of doom: "I don't want to be there when you tell her."

"Did you say on the third night of your trip? And you didn't tell me when you...?"

"Gifty, I would have loved to call you that same night from the hotel. And yes, I so much wanted to tell you immediately upon my return. But...."

"But what?"

"It's complicated."

"Complicated? How?"

Imma told her about the concerns he had shared with LuChi and Nath. He strongly expressed his love for her. He understood why the man she married had to share her faith in Jesus Christ. But he didn't want her, or anyone else, to think that he gave his life to Christ just because of that. Just because of his interest in her.

"I see. So that's why you kept this wonderful news from me? Something I've been praying for all these months? And have you told your other friends?"

"I've told LuChi and Nath. Of course, Johnny was there when it happened."

"You told LuChi and Nath? Just because they are your folks and buddies?"

Imma thought on his feet. "Haven't you heard about saving the best for last? Anyway, they are my childhood friends and they are guys. They understand what I was feeling. Just wanted their perspective in sharing my news with you. I told them with mere words. I told you in song and words – double!"

115

"Okay, I forgive you. I appreciate why you may be sensitive to what I or others think about your motive for being saved. But no such worries with me. If what we feel for each other is true love, and God wants us to spend the rest of our lives together, we still have to find out for sure in prayer. Serious prayer! This is not something I want to make a mistake about. And neither should you."

She looked at him lovingly, and took his hand. "Are you good now?"

"I am. Thank you, Gifty. You are so kind, so gracious."

"To God be the glory! Let's stop at a café and have some drinks. This calls for a celebration! I'm so happy, Imma dear!"

11

Choice worth Celebrating

What Imma didn't tell Gift, or LuChi and Nath, was the battle he had fought to summon the courage to tell his mom about Gift. Or about Mama's reaction to the news of his new faith. Or the conclusion Mama had reached about the connection between Gift and his conversion to Jesus. Or about why Imma had left home early.

Can't share any of that yet.

When the Fellowship meeting at Gift's Church ended, Tessie reminded everyone it was time for the gang's celebration of the new Imma.

"Where do you want to go, Imma?"

"I'll let Gift choose."

"Anywhere you want, as long as it's *Commint Buka or Merilyn's Kitchen,*" Gift answered, drawing laughter.

They piled into Imma's car, with Gift of course in the front seat and the other four squeezed into the back. Not too uncomfortable.

Seat belts were the only issue, but they were not likely to encounter the police.

"Tessie and I don't have seat belts on. God forgive us; we won't break the law again. Imma, it's time to change this car for a seven-seater. The gang is growing, and our kids will start coming in a few years," LuChi protested.

The gals looked at one another, and then at the guys. Tessie spoke up for them. "Is there something you guys aren't telling us? Any engagements, wedding bells?"

Nath and LuChi sat up and responded after each other for the guys.

"I suppose we're all still at the prayer stage. But doesn't the *Good Book* say that God does quick work?"

"Yes. God doesn't take forever to answer. Problem is with us, especially the gals. Some seem to take forever to hear the answer to their prayers, particularly on these matters. The King's business requires urgency."

"I agree. In two years we must have at least one junior riding in the car with us. Hence my point on a new car. But man, this cuddling and bonding is good for the soul. Close-knit is good."

Cheeky LuChi!
Dorcas, Nath's new special friend, was very beautiful and of average height like Gift and Tessie. Very light-skinned, Imma wondered if one her parents was Caucasian. She laughed a lot but had said little. She could not resist taking on LuChi, protesting on behalf of the sheltered gals.

"Close-knit? You want to enjoy touching and huddling when you haven't put a ring on the finger? Be careful."

LuChi dug in. "We have to be honest. An innocent foretaste is no sin."

"It better be innocent," Tessie warned.

Sensitive Gift must have been uncomfortable and changed the subject. "Let's go celebrate this prodigal friend of ours," she joked as they emerged from the car. "Or shall we say, ex-prodigal friend?"

"Exactly what we told him when he broke the news to us. He's like the prodigal son – lost and now found; dead and now alive." Nath let out a big laugh.

"Son of Vine, don't let this prodigal label stick."

Nath tapped Tessie and Dorcas for support. "Wouldn't that be an interesting moniker for him? We can start hailing him as Imma the ex-prodigal."

"Son of Vine, don't mind them. I hardly slept last night. Just praising the Lord and rejoicing for the new life you have found. You must already know what a treasure you've received. I'm so happy. God is good!"

The other four took turns to concur with LuChi.

Gift: "Yes, indeed. What a treasure he has found. We all have."

Tessie: "Exactly. In fact, that's the metaphor Jesus used for the experience of finding Him and entering into His kingdom. The day I gave my life to Jesus... I remember that day. The lady who spoke at the meeting told a story from the Bible that gripped me:

The Kingdom of Heaven is like a treasure hidden in a field. A wise man found the treasure buried there, and re-buried it so that no one else would find it. What a find! Ecstatic, he proceeded to sell everything he owned to raise money, and he bought that field. It's also like a jewel merchant on the hunt for the finest pearls. Finding one that was more valuable than any he had ever seen, he immediately sold all he had and bought that pearl."

This gang was surely relishing their opportunity to begin nurturing their newbie believer friend. Imma was bombarded, but indulged them.

LuChi wrapped up the session. "Indeed. And like the wise guy and jewel merchant, you will never regret what you gave up to find and have Jesus in your life – inordinate pursuit of worldly success, religion and all that."

"Thanks, all. And let me say this to you, Gifty, LuChi, Nath, Tessie and Dorcas, and as well to Johnny, Amara and Onyinye in absentia – for your love, care, and prayers to connect me and others like me to God's Kingdom: whenever my testimony is shared, you all shall get prominent mention. In fact, I learned a new song from one of the CDs I bought at the meeting where I surrendered my life to Christ. You probably know it. Can I sing it? Nobody laughs! All my life I've liked songs. I love singing. Your shaming won't stop me, anyway. I like this one very much, and have put it in my heart and my mouth, as Nath said."

Imma sang:

Thank you for giving to the Lord
I am a life that was changed
Thank you for giving to the Lord
I am so glad you gave

They all recognized Ray Boltz's *Thank You*[1] song, and joined in a portion of the last verse:

And I know up in Heaven
That you're not supposed to cry
But I'm almost sure
There were tears in your eyes
As Jesus took your hand
And you stood before the Lord
And He said My child look around you
For great is your reward

They were all wiping their eyes.

That *moment* was hardly over when Tessie showed her *Margaret Thatcher* relentlessness. She would not let go LuChi's quip about having kids, which Gift tried earlier to steer the conversation away from.

"Seriously, any engagements coming? Nath and Dorcas? Imma and Gift? I love weddings!"

"Not mine!" Gift and Dorcas exclaimed in unison.

"But I love weddings, too!" Gift added. "I like that the first miracle Jesus did was at a wedding. Oh, the sound and invitation of sweet wine. The entrance and exit music – lovely!"

LuChi didn't pass up such opportunity. "We men, too! I like that the Bible says marriage is a mystery. I like such mysteries!"

Nath added. "It's part of Heaven-on-earth experience promised believers. How does Jesus say it? 'I came that they may have and enjoy real and eternal life and have it in abundance – to the full, until it overflows.' He wants us to have a better life overall than we ever dreamed possible."

That caught Imma's attention. *Life in abundance. More than we ever dreamed possible.* "Well, I'm struggling right now with what all this means for the dream life that's so important to me and my family. Give it up?"

"No, not really. The only thing that has changed is the definition of that dream life – the source of your fulfillment."

Hearing a loud knock on another table at that moment, they all looked up.

"Forgive my interruption: Should the bill be all together, or split?"

121

The waitress! It's almost 11 pm!

"Thanks so much for the feast, guys – it's really appreciated. Let's drop off Dorcas since her home is closest. That way, we have our best chance of not being ticketed by the police."

They chattered on in the car about nothing in particular. Then LuChi blurted out. "Wait a minute, Son of Vine, don't think we'll cut you loose. You were going to tell us about your trip, the good and not-so-good. Now that we've all heard the good and celebrated it, tell us about the not-so-good."

Gift turned to Imma with concern and disappointment. "The not-so-good? You didn't mention any such thing when you told me about your trip. Imma?"

"It's not what you think."

Dorcas cut in. "Hmmm. When people say that, particularly guys, I have my concerns."

"LuChi, did you have to bring that up here? With all the ladies present?"

"No gag orders, Nath. No secrets among friends. Imma, spill it. Did you catch up with some old flame?" Tessie said, giggling.

LuChi put his hand over his mouth, his eyes darting between Nath and Imma. The genie was out of the bottle, and he attempted some face saving.

"Even if he did, remember he's born again now? Old things have passed away, and are blotted out by the blood of Jesus. Clean as a whistle!"

Gifty pushed back. "What if it was after he gave his life to Christ? Remember, after that, he went to his rural town and spent most of his vacation. Come on, Imma, I'm not jealous or anything. The Bible also says that your sin will find you out!" She laughed.

Tessie leaned forward and robbed Imma's shoulder. "Even if it was after, God's grace and forgiveness are available. And we'll forgive him, too!"

"Why are you all jumping to conclusions? Son of his father, well, I can't save you. Tell us: what's the not-so-good? It can't be that bad."

Ten eyes were on Imma and two – his – were away, distant, wrapped in another world.

Gift cajoled him. "Imma dear, what else happened?"

"Sorry, what?"

"What was the not-so-good on your trip?"

"Oh. My mom."

"What about your mom?"

Imma's fast thinking came to the rescue. How could he talk about his fight with his mom in the presence of Tessie and Dorcas? The part about Mama's allegation that Gift was responsible for his new embrace of faith in Jesus Christ would be embarrassing to Gift, and poisonous to Imma's relationship with her. Smiling wryly, Imma dodged their lure.

"That's a story for another day. It's late; let's get everyone home safely."

The last of the ladies dropped off, with the three guys on their own, LuChi apologized. "Sorry for putting you on the spot with my question. Thank God for your courage to exercise discretion."

"Yeah, I meant to talk to you two about it first. And then to Gift, alone."

"So, what is it?"

Imma shared his mom's reaction. He told them about her jumping to the conclusion that entering into a personal relationship with Jesus was only to earn Gift's hand in marriage. He explained about his rejection to join in the upcoming initiation-into-manhood ceremony, and his concern about her recent poor health.

"We had such a fight! Against her will I left home early to escape the toxic environment."

His two friends jumped right into it with candour and compassion.

"I agree. That's not so good."

"It's not good at all. I would not have cut my trip short for those reasons."

"You must be feeling bad that you left her feeling that she was the reason you ended your holiday abruptly."

"And now you've put Gift in a difficult position. Mama hasn't met Gift, and already she's thinking the worst of her."

"Yes. Gift has been thrown under the bus. Your mom will make her the fall girl for decisions that you made."

"Yeah. Just when I think this *complicated* thing is going away, it seems to become even more so."

"God can handle this. Even when things go wrong, He'll make them right."

"What are we called men and women of faith for? If God approves that Gift and you will get married, your mom is going to find Gift the most loving daughter-in-law she would ever have. And on her health, we're going to start praying for her healing. God will do it, and you and your mom will be buddies again. Don't worry!"

"We'll go visit her the next time we go home. For me, that's in the next three weeks. If she's looking for someone to heap responsibility on for your conversion, I'll tell her to fight the Holy Spirit. And if she wants to beat up a human being, I'll offer myself. I have big shoulders and strong muscles. Am I called Nath the Bulldozer for nothing?"

"And the spirit behind that sickness? We'll let it know that God is bigger than it. We'll command it to leave Mama alone. We'll expel it, and she'll be healed."

"It's going to be alright."

What great friends I have in these two, Imma thought. He voiced his appreciation and sought further counsel.

"Thanks, guys! Now, how do you think I should handle this with Gift?"

"Good question. I think you can tell her about your mom's opposition to your new faith. That's normal. But don't mention Mama's allegation that she's to blame."

"I agree. Discretion is the better part of valour."

"When both of you confirm in prayer that you are meant to get married, God will help you both win Mama over."

"And your changed life will be key to that. When she finds that what she has now is a better, more loving, more caring, responsible, and generous son, she'll become thankful for the new life we have."

"Thanks for the wise counsel. I'll find the earliest opportunity to talk to Gift about this, so she doesn't fear or suspect the worst."

"Good plan. Do that."

12

What Matters Most

Martial music and an announcement on the radio interrupted the soft Christian songs Imma was playing, jolting him from bed.

"I, Major Jehu Jedidiah of the Nigerian Army...."

It was the morning of April 22, 1990. All adults in Nigeria and other African countries knew the eerie feeling of a coup d'état. Any military overthrow of the ruling government was usually bloody. Imma put the radio to his ear – no surprise, a dawn-to-dusk curfew had been imposed throughout the country, along with the usual strong warnings to remain at home and stay calm until further instructions.

Stay calm was the part Imma would not obey today. How could he? Gift had informed him of her early-morning departure on a Church mission trip to a village on the outskirts of Lagos. If they left before the stay-at-home order, or if they didn't hear the announcement, she would be out of her home and caught up in this whirlwind coup.

On days like this Imma lamented over his country, where ninety-nine percent of the population did not have a telephone. Though richly endowed with natural resources and one of the largest exporters of oil and gas in the world, Nigeria remained embarrassingly underdeveloped. Here he was, a university graduate with a decent job who could afford a telephone, but so far he hadn't been able to get a line. Now he couldn't even call or drive over to check on Gift.

The radio on loud, Imma paced the house offering prayers every now and then for Gift's safety. He flinched when he realized he wasn't concerned for anyone except Gift. Most of his family were in the village or outside Lagos, the hotbed of coups and their ensuing violence, and should be okay. How about LuChi, Nath and other friends and colleagues? Even as he rebuked himself, included them in his prayers, and ran downstairs to check on his neighbours, it dawned on him that Gift had become the most important person in his life.

With the planned Church service today at LuChi's and Nath's Fellowship centre also overthrown by the coup, Imma had all day for some deep reflection. Thoughts started buzzing like bees in his head. He fished out his ragged, red diary and turned to the entry he had made in 1979.

> *December 5, 1979. University of Nigeria, Nsukka.*
> *No one will ever again describe me or my family as deprived. Never again!*

I've come a long way from 1979, Imma mused while re-reading the words he had written. *And, much longer from childhood and its material deprivations.* The hard labour of subsistence farming was far behind him now. Acute lack of finances has been conquered. All his siblings pursued their education with no hindrance, and his parents were provided for. He even had capacity to provide educational and medical charity outside immediate family."
Imma appreciated these strides in education. He nearly did not go to secondary school, and now he had the prospect to go to America.

Oh yes, that going-to-America dream.

Today, the dream woke up in full force. The coup, crippling curfews, and unending underdevelopment in his country brought other kinds of deprivation to the fore. Non-access to telephone service except in his office; freedoms robbed from him and his people by the military dictatorships.

In America, I'd enjoy all those things.

Lingering on the going-to-America dream, it hit him. *I haven't mentioned that to Gifty!* How would that fit into his dream to marry her? Another complication!

Imma decided to disclose the dream next time he saw her. His earlier realization that Gift was the only person he was concerned about during the coup was confirmation that he wanted to spend the rest of his life with her. He didn't know exactly how God answered prayers. But He wouldn't make her the singular focus of his love if she wasn't *the one.* Imma seized that as God's answer, and decided he would propose to Gift.

Pondering further on the twist that led him to this new path, Imma was relieved that he hadn't gone to see the doctor since he made Jesus his personal Saviour and Lord. The 'pharmacy' that LuChi had stumbled on in his home was now closed. He now attended the Full Gospel Businessmen's Fellowship in Lagos, where sharing testimonies was a hallmark. In Fellowship meetings, and with friends, colleagues and family, Imma shared that Jesus Christ's love, peace and joy had filled his life and washed away the discontentment and non-fulfillment that had plagued him and caused the fatigue and other ailments the doctors could not diagnose.

It dawned on Imma that in 1979 when he had vowed to never again be labelled as deprived, he had focused only on money and material things. While educational success, awards and career success had brought him better finances and more material possessions, these things had failed to give him peace, contentment, fulfillment, or joy. *Even with stuff, I was still deprived.* Though he continued to work hard at his job, and to pursue educational opportunities to advance his career, he couldn't remember the last time he had compared himself with others, sought to outrun others on the rat race, or lost sleep over such. As he mused over the vow, two of Jesus Christ's sayings he had learned dropped into his heart.

I came so they can have life – more abundant and better than they ever dreamed of.

I am the way, the truth, and the life.

Hmm, he thought. *The dream life?*

The Full Gospel Businessmen's Fellowship displayed the Happiest People on Earth banner at all meetings, and as everyone joined hands they ended with their anthem.

His banner over us is love
His banner over us is love
He brought us into His banqueting hall
And His banner over us is love

Imma coveted the fulfillment of the promise of that banner, and that song, in his life.

Three hours later, with more details about the coup still not available and the radio continuing to play martial music, Imma was frustrated. Was the coup successful? Would it be foiled? Was it violent, or non-violent? Some leaders of government had been killed in previous coups as the plotters upended the sitting government and consolidated power. Whenever the coup was foiled, or when the plotters failed to consolidate power and form a new government, the blood of the plotters flowed. Gestapo-style military trials always ended in public executions by firing squad. Imma hated the savagery of robbing families of sons, husbands, fathers, brothers, uncles, cousins and nephews for their association with a coup. Suspecting that a coup was being planned, or hearing a rumour but failing to report it, was enough. At best, they suffered long prison sentences.

Even many years after the bloodiest coup in Nigeria's history, Imma shivered as he recalled the aftermath of one of the executions. Convinced of her husband's innocence, the expatriate wife of a lieutenant-colonel did everything to have him exonerated. When she failed and her husband was executed, she drove her car down a slope, plunged into a river and snuffed out her life.

Imma still could not fathom how such well-publicized harrowing experiences did not dissuade coup plotters. Even as he reminisced, images that had splashed on television and newspapers over the years came rushing into his mind. Military men with legs chained, hands cuffed, and eyes empty sitting silently before military tribunals like sheep being led to slaughter. Men in the prime of life being marched to the execution grounds. Tied to the stakes. Or with heads hanging down as they succumbed to a hail of merciless bullets. As yet another coup unfolded today, Imma reached the painful conclusion that nothing would stop military men with inordinate ambition for power.

Over a late lunch, Imma's mind flipped back to the fight he had had with his mom over his new faith and Gift. And appreciated again Jesus' words addressing such conflict and promising victory.

...If you prefer father or mother over Me, you don't deserve Me. Everything I've taught you is so the peace in Me will be in you, and it will give you great confidence as you rest in Me. In this world you will have troubles and opposition. But be courageous and of good cheer, because I have overcome on your behalf.

Imma comforted himself with the belief that he would be able to patch things over with his mom. God would give him wisdom, and LuChi and Nath had promised to support him. If Gift agreed to marry him, Imma was sure that his mom would come to accept and love Gift. He did not, however, kid himself that it would be an easy road – with his mom, his elder siblings, extended family and some friends. He braced himself to accept Jesus' warning of troubles, and to position himself to enjoy His promise of peace and victory.

Imma woke up the next day to a radio announcement. The coup had been foiled, and people should go about their normal business. He hurriedly went to work with a detour to Gift's home. Multiple checkpoints by soldiers in full combat gear littered the roads and brought traffic to a near standstill. Imma should have remembered. The days following every coup, whether successful or foiled, usually saw heavy security everywhere as soldiers hunted escaping coup plotters or toppled government officials. Everything in him screamed to confirm that Gift was fine, but at this snail speed he could not make it to her home and still get to work on time. He said a quick prayer and decided he would call her office first thing on getting to work.

Imma might as well not have gone to work that day. Several calls to Gift's office went unanswered, and he could hardly focus. He left work an hour early and found all the shortcuts to Gift's office. Gift was not there. After a frantic plea, the receptionist disclosed that Gift was working at one of the bank's branches that day. Weaving his way through the heavy-security traffic, Imma prayed to get to Gift's location before it closed.

He caught her in a bear hug as she stepped out of the door. "Thank God you're okay!"

"I'm glad you are, too."

"When I couldn't reach you yesterday and at the office today I was so worried…"

"Oh, how caring!" Gift explained that they hadn't heard about the coup until they returned to Lagos from their mission trip. Thankfully, soldiers at the checkpoints had accepted their explanation for being out. She had forgotten to mention to Imma that she would not be working out of head office that day.

Imma drove Gift home, and stayed for dinner. Afterward, he invited her for a walk. Outside the house, Imma bought two cans of her favourite soft drink. Seeking privacy, they sat in his car.

"You look serious."

"This is an important talk. Hope I don't look nervous."

"Should you be?"

"I don't know."

Adjusting his seating position several times, he fidgeted with the car keys. With Gift's eyes bearing down his soul, he finally leaned against the car window facing her squarely.

"First: on the not-so-good things that happened at home, my apologies that I haven't shared those. I wasn't trying to hide anything; just wanted to find the right time."

When he shared his mom's negative reaction to his decision to enter into a personal relationship with Jesus, Gift took it in stride.

"I'm not surprised. It's common. I was fortunate that my parents didn't raise any serious objections, but that's the exception. Don't worry, your mom loves you. She won't disown you, as in the worst cases we've heard. The Bible says that by our fruits people will know us. It's on you to prove to her that she now has a better son because of your personal relationship with Jesus."

"Exactly what LuChi and Nath said."

"You have told them then?"

"Yes. Last night, after we dropped off Tessie and Dorcas. My plan was to tell you three only."

"You said you had a few things tugging at your heart. What more?"

"Two more things."

Imma took a long sip of his drink.

"Remember when I told you that there was just one more box that I needed to check to fully settle down?"

"I do."

"I lied."

"You lied?"

"You know what I mean. I forgot to list all the unchecked boxes. I omitted one. Maybe then wasn't the right time, but now is."

Imma told her about his going-to-America dream – how it was sown in his heart out of nowhere; how providential he thought it was: God using his godfather, Professor Godson. After barely making it to secondary school, he now had an opportunity for graduate studies and work in God's own country, the United States of America!

"You had challenges going to secondary school? You couldn't pass the entrance exam? And to think I've considered you a smart person all this while," Gift said, laughing.

"Not that, I can hold my own. The day you finally come to my house, my award plaques will reassure you that the guy chasing after you is not a dummy."

"So how come you almost missed getting a secondary school education?"

"You're tricking me into disclosing the most personal things about my life. Hearer beware: I've always said that the lady who hears this has to be *the one*."

"We have already agreed that it is in God's hands. We are still praying about *the one*, aren't we? Maybe part of that is getting to know each other better. Go ahead and tell me."

Feeling safe with Gift and confident in a possible future together, Imma gathered courage to turn over the pages of his life from the beginning, and give her a complete portrait - his struggle with farming, his parents' financial constraint to put him through both secondary school and university and the people God used to overcome that. As well, he shared the one he was yet to be fully rescued from – the 'deprived' child label.

"Still vivid in my mind is the day I received the admission letter posting me to Madonna High School, Etiti. Jumping up and down and screaming like I had never done in my twelve years of life then, I ran home to share it with my parents especially."

"They must have been very proud. From what I heard, Madonna was a tough school to get into in those days "

"Yeah, it was. And my parents seemed pleased, with my dad's 'Good job son!', and my mom's 'Well-done, father of my husband, you make us proud!'"

"Is that what your mom calls you?" Gift asked

"Yes, when she was happy with me. When she wasn't, what she called me…I wouldn't repeat," Imma answered laughing.

"I know some people believe in reincarnation – did they say you're your granddad's…?"

"Oh no. May be I reminded her of my grandfather."

"Anyway, to continue the story, they fooled me with that expression of pride, because the next morning they delivered the blow."

Gift drew close. "Blow?"

"You may be aware of those early morning meetings where elders deliver hard news. My parents woke me and said I wouldn't be taking up the admission."

"What? Why?"

"My mom opened the conversation with that 'father of my husband' call name, and after reiterating their pride for my accomplishment, nudged my dad to tell me. I still remember his shaky voice: 'Imma, your mom and I would love nothing more than see you take up this admission. And we have tried everything so far to save money and ensure that you can go. However, school fees went up for your five older siblings. We can't afford to send an extra child to secondary school. At least not this year.'"

"That was bad, hard news!"

"There was worse. My mom ever the pragmatist and sharp shooter, jumped in. 'The father of my husband. I know it looks bad, but that's the reality. We have made enquiries about getting you a place to learn auto mechanic. And if by next year our finances improve and school fees for your siblings don't go up you can get into secondary school."

"Oh my God!" Gift said, and covered her mouth.

"I was not prepared for that at all. I believe my older siblings knew of my parents' decision but didn't alert me. The previous night they hushed and stared when I came close "

Gift, ever the benefit-of-the-doubt giving, kind person, defended them.

"They didn't want to break your heart."

"Or, my mom asked them to zip it. But they could have prepared their little brother to take the blow better."

"Forgive them. So, how did the miracle happen?"

"As you can imagine, my world collapsed with that news. Accusing them of unfairness in sending the older five to secondary school and leaving me, banging doors, looking myself in the mirror to confirm that I was who they said I was – their son -, didn't help. When the cock crowed every morning following, they still dragged me up to go to the farm or stream. The admission wasn't mentioned and I lost the hope of escaping the village and farming hard life.

"But three weeks later, my cousin Mark visited and offered to take me with him to Makurdi where he worked. Gifty, he financed my secondary school education.

"So, there you have it…"

At that point Imma looked away, rubbing his eyes.

Gift offered a handkerchief and held his hand. "I'm so sorry. I can't imagine how traumatic it was for you going through all that. But it's all good now."

"Yeah, thank God," Imma said, forcing a smile.

"But seriously, I'm trying to imagine you in a blue coverall and underneath a car – as a renowned auto mechanic." Gift let out a big laughter.
"Would have made sure I found you still, to become your personal auto mechanic," Imma said, joining the laughter.

"Where would you have met me? Not living in that your remote village. Anyway, we bless God. Your aspirations to go to secondary school and university have been actualized. You have a great career. God has been good to you, and it's great that His goodness has led you to repentance; to a personal relationship with Him through faith in Jesus Christ. You are not a deprived child! "

"I've heard that line before."

"What line?"

"God's goodness leads to repentance. From LuChi. You all talk alike."

"It's not just a line. It's a truth from God's Word. It's His promise to all people. He wants to do good to everyone, to show them unconditional love. He desires that all will be drawn to embrace the abundant and eternal life that Jesus came to give."

"I am glad for His goodness. I'm happy that I've been led to make Jesus my Saviour and Lord. But going to America should be part of the abundant life – an escape from the deprived life."

"Your going-to-America dream, it's really interesting."

"How do you mean?"

"Have you thought about timing? And how does it align with your other unchecked box – marriage?"

"Yeah, I've thought about that, but have no clue yet how they'll all come together."

"One way to find out – prayer. Now that you're a child of God, you can ask for His counsel and the Holy Spirit will order your steps."

"I'm going to be doing a lot of praying, it seems."

"Don't let it weigh you down. Prayer is simply a conversation between you and our Heavenly Father through Jesus Christ. Based on His promises to you in the Bible, it shouldn't be burdensome."

"I've heard that before too. Johnny told me. Thanks for the counsel – I can sure have conversations with God. And I can trust that I hear Him clearly."

"That's right – trust that you hear Him. It's all by faith."

"Do you have a plan for going to graduate school? Here or overseas?"

"As you know, my parents schooled and lived in England; and my two brothers now live there. It looks to me that living abroad is in God's plan for me, but I'm not sure of the timing yet."

"That makes two of us. I'm happy for one more common interest."

"Don't get ahead of yourself. Just keep praying."

Imma didn't know all the ways that prayers – conversations with God – are heard or answered. But if the ring of Gift's voice and the sunny smile on her face were anything to go by, the answer to *the one* prayer seemed on its way. By faith!

He saw her home and jumped back into the car, conversing with God and smiling all the way home.

13

The Tide is High but I'm Holding On

The moment Gift told Imma that she had scheduled a party at her sister's home to mark her twenty-third birthday, his mind went into overdrive. *Kairos. Seize the moment!* Her first social event since they became friends. Lots of her other friends and family would be there, and Imma wanted to make an appearance. As *the one* to-be. Well, if there were any other contenders for her highest affection, they had to know who was number one. His heart sank as he remembered that Gift was still praying about it. What if she came back with a negative answer to her prayers?

Driving to pick up LuChi early that warm vacation afternoon for the evening party, Imma slotted in one of his old music collections and sang along to a song by the Paragons, *The Tide is High*[2].

> *The tide is high but I'm holding on*
> *I'm gonna be your number one*
> *I'm not the kind of man who gives up just like that*
> *Oh, no…!*

Raising his voice each time it got to the 'Oh, no' part, he gripped the steering hard and imagined both Gift and God nodding their heads in confirmation, convinced of his genuine love and impressed with his determination.

"Son of Vine, you are pulling no punches! That's a lovely blazer you're spotting. Blue is your hue, man! Hope you don't outdo the birthday gal and steal her show."

"I'm alright, then? This is an important stage for me today."

"I know. And you are ready to go with your special song?"

"Ready as can be!"

"Let's have a rehearsal."

Imma impressed LuChi with a flawless rendition of his surprise birthday song for Gift – one of the many songs he had recently learned at the Full Gospel Businessmen's Fellowship meetings. He was going to one-up every other person with both a speech and a song in tribute to Gift. He prayed to score some brownie points.

Gift was resplendent in a flowing yellow velvet dress as she answered the door and hugged LuChi and Imma. A whiff of her favourite Elizabeth Arden Red Door perfume caressed Imma's nostrils. It always wore well on her, just as her birthday dress and new hairdo did today. Imma and LuChi were early arrivals and they quickly went to work helping set up the cake, gifts and music tables.

They gingerly sat the modest cake covered in royal marigold icing and decorated with pink roses in the middle of the table. A beautiful glass vase held a candle and a wooden stick with the number 23 at the top.

"I thought girls didn't disclose their age."

"Not this one! I like to celebrate my life, and I'm proud to acknowledge the beautiful years God has given me so far."

Imma was sure that Gift hadn't appointed LuChi to the role of master of ceremonies, but LuChi didn't need to be appointed. A take-charge, get-things-done type of guy, he was soon putting on soft music and dragging Imma to join in welcoming the guests. Imma was engaged in the party, but also watching from the corner of his eyes all the guys who streamed in. After all, he had also learned that the Bible admonished to watch and pray.

Food and drinks served, LuChi called on Gift to cut the cake. He led everyone in singing a birthday song:

> *Happy birthday to you*
> *All glory to God*
> *May long life be your portion*
> *Happy birthday to you!*

Imma had never heard it sung that way before.

"Now we want to open the floor to anyone who has one or two things to say in celebration of the life of our birthday girl."

A few people spoke – friends and members of her Church. When there were no more volunteers to pay tribute to Gift, Imma was glad that it had been all speech and no song. Now it was his turn to seize the moment.

"I know one more person here has something to say – or to sing," announced LuChi. "Imma, the floor is yours."

Suddenly the room seemed larger. He was not used to speaking in front of such a big crowd, let alone singing. All the singing he had ever done was to himself, or anonymously in Church. The rehearsal with LuChi this afternoon had been a first, and it had been to just one person. Imma walked to the centre of the room, his knees shaking. After paying his compliments to Gift, he began to sing in her honour:

> *Let Your living water flow over my soul*
> *Let Your Holy Spirit come and take control*

Of every situation that has troubled my mind
All my cares and burden unto You I roll
Father, Father, Father!

Give your life to Jesus, let Him fill your soul
Let Him take you in His arms and make you whole
As you give your life to Him, He'll set you free,
You will live and reign with Him eternally.
Jesus, Jesus, Jesus!

Then it happened. The last stanza evaporated from Imma's mind. He opened his mouth several times, but nothing came out. Nothing. Cold sweat began to run down under his shirt. Imma wished the ground would open, swallow him up and rid him of this misery, but it didn't.

Catching on, LuChi jumped up and joined Imma. Putting his arms round his shoulder, he sang the last stanza.

Come now Holy Spirit and take control
Hold me in Your loving arms and make me whole
Wipe away all doubt and fear and take my pride
Draw me to Your love and keep me by Your precious side.
Spirit, Spirit, Spirit[3]!

When the song was completed to rousing applause, Imma went straight to the bathroom. What if LuChi hadn't been with him at this party? *A friend in need is a friend indeed* had never held more meaning for him.

Imma had enjoyed a few major rescues in his life: the rescue from going to learn a trade instead of getting a secondary school education. The rescue from not taking up his university admission. The rescue from not being disqualified for the New Nigeria bank job because he wasn't an indigene of the owner-state. And the salvation from a life devoid of joy, peace, fulfillment and passion. This rescue today by LuChi ranked right up there.

142

And what was the round of applause for? Did people think it was planned for LuChi to join Imma to complete the song? Imma was quiet, sitting by himself for the rest of the party. In her appreciation speech Gift had put her hand on her chest and expressed how touched she was by his song, but Imma couldn't wait to go home. He had made a fool of himself and feared that Gift was just being polite. *How much higher has the tide become?*

In the following weeks, Imma held on and looked for every opportunity to undo his mess. He joined her to church services, enjoyed weekend social outings with their mutual friends and sent her beautiful, romantic cards - special occasion or not. *Just no singing!*

Their relationship progressed well and Imma's confidence grew. Eleven months since he knew Gift, the time had come to take their friendship to the next level - meet her parents and introduce her to his. Especially to his Mom! The soon-coming Christmas was the perfect time, and being from the same Imo State, they agreed to travel home together.

December 22, 1989, Lagos.

At 4 am Imma was bright-eyed, loading up luggage in his cousin's gold-coloured Mercedes Benz 190 saloon. In fifteen minutes, he was at Gift's Femi Ayantuga Street, Surulere home.

"You have a new car?"

"No. My cousin in the US sent this for his convenience whenever he is in Nigeria. He said I could use it – he doesn't want it to rust from being parked too long."

"You're not trying to impress me or my family?" Gift asked, laughing.

"Are you impressed?"

"Mercedes Benz is a great luxury car, but you should be content with your Nissan Bluebird. I just assumed we'd be riding in it today, that's all."

Caught in the act, Imma was embarrassed and needing to do damage control. "Don't worry," he quipped, "we'll ride in my car next time. Or yours."

By 5 am they had picked up Gift's girlfriend and university classmate who would be spending Christmas with her, and were well on their way. Christmas saw the heaviest traffic on the Lagos-Owerri route. People from their part of the country had a tradition of mass exodus from the big cities where they worked, and the eight-hour journey easily extended to twelve or fourteen hours. With traffic snarls from too many vehicles, and an unreasonable number of police checkpoints used more for extorting money than providing order and security, it was not uncommon for people to get to their homes at midnight. Imma was glad for their early start.

Focused on dropping off Gift and her friend at Owerri and still making the additional drive to his village the same night, Imma maintained good speed. The trio chatted away excitedly and shared snacks with Christmas carols playing softly on the stereo. Two hours into the drive Imma looked in the rear view mirror and saw smoke wisping up from the back of the car. Unfamiliar with diesel motors, he hoped it was normal for them to emit smoke.

His heart sank when the smoke turned into a billowing cloud, the wind blowing it all the way to the front. Still hoping that it was nothing, and that Gift and her friend wouldn't notice, he sped on.

Huge mistake. A crackling noise emerged from the engine.

"What's that noise?"

Imma continued to be in denial. "Not sure; it should be nothing. This car was supposed to be in top condition."

"Wise to stop and check it out."

By this time the swelling mass of smoke was surging into the cabin, and the car was decelerating. Imma, drenched in cold sweat, parked by the side of the road and turned off the ignition.

It had been six months since he had embarrassed himself at Gift's birthday. And now this! If only LuChi or Nath was with him, they could make the landing less hard. Imma was on his own. But the ground didn't open for him to disappear.

Opening the hood, he took a deep breath and leaned into the car.

"I'm sorry, ladies, but it looks like something in the engine is fried."

They came out of the car, worry written on their faces.

Gift took his hand. "What are we going to do?"

A car pulled up in front of them. It was a man from Imma's neighbouring village, on his way home for Christmas as well. Jointly assessing the situation, they agreed it was best for Imma to tow the car back to Lagos. The guy had two spaces in his car and offered to take Gift and her friend to Owerri.

Imma waved them off, kicking the tires of the Mercedes Benz and swearing to never try to impress with what didn't belong to him. Never again!

Two hours later the tow truck dumped the Mercedes Benz at Imma's Lagos home. Back on his way to Owerri, he demanded more from his old, reliable Nissan Bluebird than he had ever done before. Mercifully, it obliged him with speed, efficient gas consumption, and no breakdowns.

Arriving at Owerri at 9 pm, he headed straight for Gift's home. She would be concerned about how he had fared. But what was important to him was salvaging some of his pride. He didn't impress her with the borrowed Mercedes Benz. But wouldn't she give him some points for the great recovery?

Not how often you fall down, but whether you get up each time!

Unfamiliar with the city, and with most streets and homes without electricity in thick darkness, Imma threw away embarrassment and caution, stopping people on the road and knocking on homes to help him find Gift's home. His prayer was answered when a man who knew Gift's dad gave Imma directions.

Mission accomplished. Just by showing his face and promising to visit the next day. Imma headed to his village.

Letting out a big yawn, Imma dragged himself out of bed at 11 am that December 23. He hurried with unloading and presenting to his mom the special Christmas gifts - bags of rice, tins of tomato paste, gallons of vegetable oil and a large bale of stockfish.

"The father of my husband, welcome again!

"Thank you Mama. Those are for you. I'll give money to purchase gifts for the extended family in the local market. There's only so much that can fit in a car."

"You have done very well."

Imma excused himself to do the greeting rounds with the extended family, rejoicing that Mama was warm and seemed very pleased. *Hopefully she's that way when I bring Gifty.* A few hours later, he was on his way to Owerri, the home of Gifty's parents, praying all the way and hoping.
The heavy traffic of the Christmas season already building up, it took Imma two hours – double the normal drive - to reach there.

Gifty answered the door.

"So glad you made it home safe. When did you get there?"

"Just before midnight. Thankfully, lots of cars on the road still. One of the great things about this season."

"Hello. That's the Imma of last night?" Gift's dad asked, rising from his armchair, clutching a newspaper in one hand and extending the other.

Imma bowed, and with two hands shook the extended hand. "Yes sir. My honour to meet you, sir!" Almost 6 foot, he was ebony black, dignified and strong – every inch the overseas trained Engineering Director. *That's where Gifty got her complexion and nose!*

Gift's mom, a secondary school teacher, emerged. Gift's height and sprightliness and Sharon's light skin are from their mom.

"Oh, welcome! Now we can meet you – we hardly saw your face before you took off last night. You should have passed the night here, it was late."

"Thanks so much *Ma'*. It wasn't a problem, the road was safe."

Gift's parents gave Imma more hospitality than he could wish. He wasn't surprised – Sharon and Gift came from that stock!

"Imma, time to go home! You're not getting any excuse to sleep here tonight or get home at midnight again," Gift announced, laughing.
"Why are you chasing him away?" Gift's oldest sister, Ada, and youngest, Nwadiuto who also lived in Owerri, chorused.

"She's right, I shouldn't overstay my welcome," Imma answered, chuckling. "The traffic was bad as I drove up here and must have gotten worse. Don't want to make my mom or yourselves worried about me again."

Securing Gift's agreement to visit his home with Nwadiuto who, Imma scheduled to pick them up in a few days.

The traffic snarl failed to dampen Imma's joy as he drove home! There were three more Gift's siblings to meet – two living overseas - and Imma betted that they would be nice and welcoming, too.

Turning his mind to his family, Imma began to plot how to get Mama to be even half as nice…

December 27 could not come early enough for Imma. Unsure that he had lobbied his dad and coaxed his mom enough, he was ready to show off Gifty.

Getting home, Imma's parents were away at the Village centre for a community project fund-raising event. For his siblings, it was love at first sight for Gift, and they matched Gift's family's reception. And then, Imma drove with her and Nwadiuto to the Village square and sent for his parents.

His dad was first to come out.

"Welcome my daughters. How are your parents?"

"They are fine, sir. Happy Christmas, sir!" Gift and Nwadiuto chorused.

Imma's mom joined.

"Welcome! Sorry we are not home. Imma I hope your sisters gave them food?"

"Yes Ma'; they fed us very full. Happy Christmas Ma',"

"Same to you. Imma, which one is Gift?"

Imma took Gift's hand, drawing her close and beaming.

"Mama, this is Gift. And that's her sister, Nwadiuto."

"Beautiful children!"

"Thank you Ma'"

"I have heard so much about you, Gift." Mama quipped.

Papa quickly added, "Very good things!"

Imma breathed a quiet sigh of relief.

"I hear also that your father is Obioha, the Doctor?"

"Yes, Ma'"

"Very nice man. We know about him."

Imma's dad jumped in.

"Yes, very good family! Welcome again. We have to go back to the bazaar. Imma I hope you'll all join us?"

"Yes, they have to, so we can see Gift and her sister at home after. Imma, they have called your name severally already to make your donation."

"No, they are going back to Owerri and I don't want to drive in the night. Mama, here's my donation – please make it on my behalf."

Imma's parents hugged Gift and Nwadiuto. "Greet your parents and please come again."

Christmas and New Year festivities over, an elated Imma drove back to Lagos. On this trip he had enjoyed yet more rescue in his life. An image of Gift and her friend picking their luggage from that engine-knocked Mercedes Benz and hopping into a tow truck with him crossed his mind. *That would have been a nightmare!*

Gift's parents and siblings had been wonderful and accepting. Some of his family had now met and loved Gift and the ice was broken with his mom! It was still work in progress with her. She recognized Gift's respected family name, seemed to like her, and neither confronted her nor again allege that Gift converted her son to Faith.

I'll take that.

Round two won.

14

Where the Broken Road Leads

This was going to be one special Saturday evening.

Buoyed by the answer to the prayer for *the one* he believed he had received, and the positive feedback from the introduction to the families, Imma knew he had to strike while the iron was hot. Whether Gift had got her own answer, and what that answer was, were outside his control and he refused to let that stop him. His part was to pop the question. Though he was hopeful, the answer would be what it would be.

"The year has gotten off to such a busy start, and we haven't had a good outing since we got back. Let's have one today."

"What do you have in mind?"

"Go somewhere we've not gone before, and have a good meal. I'm tired of all those mom and pop restaurants and fast food places we go to all the time. Let's try something different."

"I'd like that! Novelty is welcome! Where?"

"You'll decide. I'll drive to a few places and whichever you choose will be it."

Imma knew where he wanted to go for this special occasion, and headed there. If Gift chose it, that would be a good sign!

Thirty minutes later they were in a highbrow part of Lagos. As he steered into the exit, Gift recognized it.

"The Sheraton Hotel Restaurant! That's it!"

"Why, you don't want to see the other cool places on my list?"

"No. You had me at number one! I've always wanted to check out this restaurant!"

"Great. I hope I get rewarded for being the one to make it happen."

"Don't get ahead of yourself. But I compliment you for your good taste." She took his hand and squeezed it affectionately.

"I'll take that for now," Imma said, laughing.

Beaming with smiles as they got seated, Imma assessed that he hadn't given away the special occasion so far. But Gift was smart. Was she just playing along?

Dinner was served by candlelight. Imma talked much more than usual, to so engage Gift that she wouldn't notice that only their table had the special lighting and decorations.

Over dessert he changed subjects. Gift could have heard the pounding of his heart, if not for his chatter.

"Posh places like this remind me of what I've been labouring for all my life."

"And what's that?"

"To escape deprivation and enjoy the good life. Glad for how far I've come."

Gift reached out and tapped his hand. "I'm happy for you!"

"Thanks Gifty. I know it is said that if I have nothing but Jesus, I'm not missing anything; that I'm not actually deprived of anything."

"Correct."

Imma took a sip of his vanilla flavour *Maltina.*

"However, I've come to understand also that He is the giver of every good and perfect thing. I want every good thing He gives; every blessing He has promised to bestow."

Gift gazed at him. "Me too. Where are you going with this sermon?"

"I'll count myself short if I'm deprived of what I consider the best gift God can give me, apart from salvation."

"What's that?"

Imma got down on one knee, fished out a golden box and flipped it open to reveal a beautiful ring. Then he did it.

"Gifty, will you marry me?"

His eyes were unsure and pleading, and he continued. "I've got my answer: you are *the one.* I love you more than any person or thing in this world. I want to spend the rest of my life with you. I want to live the abundant life with you!"

Hands clasped over her chest, she looked at him for what seemed like eternity.

Steadying himself, Imma tightened his hold on the ring box - with two hands. *Dropping that would be bad omen.*

He stammered. "Gifty, I want you to be my husband. I want to be your wife..."

"You want me to be your wife?"

"That's what I said."

She stared, released one hand from her chest and covered her mouth.

Now very concerned, Imma sought to sweeten the proposal. A poem he learned years back bubbled up from his heart.

"Gifty, *we have come to the cross-roads*
And I must either leave or come with you.
I lingered over the choice
But in the darkness of my doubts
You lifted the lamp of love
And I saw in your face
The road that I should take[4]."

Finally, she said it. "Yes, I will – I got my answer too. You are *the one*!"

Imma slipped the ring on her finger. Unmindful of prying eyes, they entered into a long, warm embrace, wetting each other's faces with mingled tears of joy.

"I'm so happy! I love you!"

"My joy is full! I'm no longer deprived! I love you more!"

They were still on cloud nine as they drove home.

"That poem, it was such sweet and compelling icing on the cake."

"Glad you liked it. Know it?"

"Yes. Kwesi Brew's *The Mesh*. One of my favourites."

"Disappointed. Half-hoped you'd think it (acknowledgement / fair use ref.) was an original – my special composition for you," Imma said with a guffaw.

"Glad it wasn't another song," she teased, laughing.

"Me too. Stake too high for a repeat of the birthday disaster."

They each shared how they had received their answer.

"The first day I saw you my heart swirled. And ever since, it has skipped almost every time I thought of you or saw you."

"So there have been days when it didn't skip?" Gift asked with a serious, concerned face.

"A few, actually. Those days after I upset you with something I said or did. Maybe my heart did skip, but with trepidation that you'd break up our relationship, rather than with excitement and love."

"I feel better now. Continue your story."

"I thought I knew already from those early days that you were *the one*. But then Nath, LuChi and you said that I had to hear from God. On the day of the coup, with nowhere to go and having all that free time, I prayed for you. And thought deeply about you. I didn't hear an audible voice from God, but I realized that I cared for you more than anyone else in the world. I seized that as my answer. I told God I believed that was my answer, and I didn't hear a no. I had peace!" Imma laughed with joy.

"God will take that. Peace is one of the ways He gives us confirmation. And I will take that, too. Or rather, I've taken that as the right answer since I already said yes." She laughed in turn.

155

"And you got your own answer how? Being a more mature Believer, I'm thinking it's something more sophisticated?"

"Interestingly, I got my confirmation the day after the coup."

Gift relayed how she had struggled with accepting that Imma could be *the one*. Candidly, Imma didn't fit the picture she had of her knight in shining armour. Initially, she saw him as a friend of her cousin James. When Imma started visiting without James, and persisted, she didn't mind being just a friend. But certainly not *the one*. She had agonized over this in prayer, and was willing to submit to God's approval if He showed her a clear sign.

"I still prayed after the coup, and I heard the Lord say, 'You will see him at work today.' I wondered about that. I didn't tell you or any other guy that I would be at the branch office that day. Was I going to meet someone new there? Anyway, my concern that I might have misheard God vanished when I was told I had a visitor, and it turned out to be you. I knew I had my confirmation."

Imma released one hand from the steering wheel and squeezed Gift's, smiling broadly. "Wow! I actually thought of going to your home that day to await your return from work. I'm so glad I followed the Invisible Hand that led me instead to your branch office! 'God bless the broken road that led me straight to you'. Round three won!"

"Round three?"

"Round one – your friendship. Round two – family acceptance. Round three – the yes."

"It's not a fight!"

"I just like to measure my progress."

156

Hanging out with Gift a week later at Sharon's home, Imma cleared his throat. "We have the yes, we have the family acceptance and we have the money. What's stopping us?"

"From what?"

"Getting married!"

"You tell me."

"Nothing."

"You're not forgetting something?"

"What?"

Gift peered at Imma. He looked sideways, tapping his head.

"Can't think of anything. Don't give me a hard time. What do you think I'm forgetting?"

"Your going-to-America dream."

"Oh, that."

They launched into a full-blown evaluation. The dream was desirable still, but it didn't have same grip on Imma anymore as the ultimate way to escape the deprived life and attain the dream life.

"I've found life in Jesus Christ – abundant life, eternal life. And I've found you. I'm fulfilled. I'm content."

"I just don't want to be blamed in the future as the reason you didn't fulfill a dream you've spoken so strongly about."

"It's now a nice-to-have. We can join your dream to mine and pursue it together – studying and living overseas. Just both of us, or with our kids."

"You're getting ahead of yourself." She paused. "Again!"

"Guilty as charged. But I always catch up! I can see our kids already, and we'll have them!" Imma winked at her, took her hand, and squeezed it longingly.

In the next few weeks they began putting together a roadmap to their big day. The wedding. Imma wrote it all down in his ragged, red diary and had Gift read it out.

Formally inform our families, and obtain Gift's parents' consent. Obtain dates for the traditional marriage rites, climaxing in the traditional wedding.
Perform the government registry marriage.
Seal and celebrate it all with the Church wedding.
Accomplish all in six months.'

"Agree?"

"Agree."

They prayed for God's wisdom and help. The next rounds had to be won. And then the ultimate prize.

Participation in the wedding feast of The Lamb, Jesus, in Heaven.

Growing up, Imma did not have his share of the luxuries of life. He had made progress enjoying a semblance of them – middle-class job, car, home, helping his family. But there was another dream he hadn't shared with Gift or anybody else – that his wedding would be a showpiece for what it means to not be deprived. Spare no expense. Exquisite wedding gown for his bride, and top-of-the-range suit for himself, ordered from overseas. Church service in a cathedral, and wedding reception in a posh hotel. Make a statement.

They decided to find a place of worship to call their home Church in addition to being active in the Full Gospel Businessmen's Fellowship. They prayerfully settled on Jesus Life Chapel. Their worship centre still under construction in a non-developed, grassy, water-logged part of Lagos, the building looked like a sheep pen. The Pastor advised that he would understand if they chose to hold the wedding service elsewhere.

Gift's two siblings lived in England, but Imma wasn't about to begin so soon to ask them for wedding apparel favours. He hadn't even met them. Fortunately, his oldest sister, her family and his two older brothers now lived and schooled in the US. When they offered to send the dream wedding gown and suit as their gift, Imma considered those items checked off the list.

Until he got the call from his oldest sister in America, Adaoma.

"Imma, congrats in advance on your wedding."

"Thanks *Dada*. How are you all doing?"

"Okay. But what's this we hear about where wedding service venue."

"Since I gave my life to Christ I've got a new home church and that's where we'll wed."

"Have you gone crazy? We have a family religion and everyone before you has wedded there. What makes you think you're different?"

"*Dada*, well, it's just where Gift and I would be happy…"

"Please stop. I disagree with you and I'm sure the rest of the family as well. Don't cause any unnecessary heartache with this stupid fanaticism."

Imma began a spirited case to defend his position. At that same moment, he heard *click*.

Within a few days the opposition to his new faith became a headwind, swirling into a perfect storm into which Imma ran headlong. His mom and siblings in the US insisted that he go back to the family religion. The wedding became a perfect opportunity to force him to do their bidding. Imma conveyed his respect for their views, pleading with them to do the same for his decision. About two weeks before the wedding the matter had still not been resolved. Imma's brother-in-law suggested a compromise: wed in his family place of worship, then go back to his new church afterward.

Concerned that her marrying into the family would cause a rift, Gift pleaded with Imma to accept the compromise. Imma politely declined.

"This is the most important ceremony in my life and I want to be happy. Holding it in a forced location will be a pretense. I will not be miserable at my wedding!"

The negotiations broke down irreparably and the *Americana*'s threw down the gavel.

"Have it your way Imma, but you won't be getting any wedding gown and suit from us. Sorry."

Before Imma recovered to protest, the phone clicked. *Again!*

Imma broke into a panic. When he eventually found courage to tell Gifty, he wasn't sure what to expect.

"Imma dear, what are we going to do?"

"Will figure something out, Gifty."

"Please don't let your stubbornness ruin my wedding."

"Nothing and no one can ruin our wedding. Trust me."

"I do. 'Am praying you're right. Otherwise…" She left the house.

That night sleep deserted Imma. He lay in bed agonizing and praying over the situation. He discovered in his core that this wasn't just about a wedding venue, gown and suit. In essence, it was about his life. It was about what would give him abiding peace and fulfillment. *Make our joy full.* Esteeming dignity and independence over dream wedding apparel, Imma resolved to not reach out to other contacts overseas or in Nigeria for that favour.

Their special day finally came.

Wading through the narrow marshy road that had been shored up with stones, the driver of the courtesy car from Imma's bank got him and his best man Nath to the church early.

Nath, with his Accounting designation in the bag and now an Auditor in a reputable firm, didn't pull punches.

"You probably should have listened to the suggestion to hold this service at the reception venue. Many of your guests could get stuck on that road."

Imma shrugged. "We made it; they'll make it alright. Members of the church are handy to give a pushing hand if required."

"No one will forget ever attending your wedding."

Imma laughed, in very high spirits. "Memorial is a good thing"

"Forgive me, but it's not just because of the road. I hear people have nick-named your worship building a cowshed. Many more will make that name famous after today."

"No apology needed. Jesus was born in a manger" Imma retorted, letting out a bigger laugh.

Nath took a good look at his friend and gave him a thumbs up.

"I like your faith."

"I have good mentors!"

Leaving the car air-conditioning running, the driver ensured that Imma and Nath were comfortable as they waited. Peeping at their watches and stealing a glance at each every few minutes, both called out to people to check when they would be called in. Thirty minutes past the service start time turned into an hour, and the delay was revealed: Gift's party had not arrived.

Officiating minister and Jesus Life Chapel pastor, Chima, came by.

"Has Gift changed her mind?"

Imma laughed. "No way! Saw her late last night and she was making her hair promising to look even more beautiful for me."

"She can't afford to stand up this handsome man, can she? It must be the traffic, Pastor," Nath added, supporting.

"I believe you. Just checking," Pastor Chima said, laughing as he went back to the church.

"Seriously, how are you doing, son of his father?"

"Nath the bulldozer, if I were any better, I'd be twins!"

"Sure? Just doing my job as best man."

"I know. I'm fine. Gift will be here soon. The driver picking her must have shown up late or traffic is worse than usual."

"I believe you."

"Lots of people say that to me. They better mean it!"

"You are very believable." They both laughed.

Imma changed the subject.

"This is all surreal."

"What?"

"I'm getting married!" Imma hollered, and continued.

"I told you about my red diary and the very first entry?"

Nath stared at him searchingly.

"Yes. It's been over eleven years! Don't tell me you're still obsessed with that 'deprived children' talk?"

"It's been the rocket fuel and reference point for me. Just last night I was sharing with Gifty the questions that still creep up in my heart about totally escaping that label."

"We've talked about that…"

"Yes. I can't help wondering sometimes whether I'm on the right path or if this dream life – abundant life? – is just chasing after the wind."

"And what did Gifty say?"

Just then they came to usher them into the service. Gifty had arrived.

Imma pumped the air and lifted his hands as he alighted. "Yes! Praise The Lord!"

Resplendent and graceful in the simple emergency wedding dress they bought, Gift's eyes caught Imma's as her party danced to live praise music to the altar. Standing and beaming with the purest smile in an old suit he dry-cleaned, Imma was on top of the world.

They couldn't be happier for all the family, friends and colleagues who graced the occasion. Umunna, Chukwuemeka, Iwunze, Chuma, Matt, Adelana, Jeff… they were all there. Restless LuChi who recently took a position as Assistant Editor of *TSM* (The Sunday Magazine), was the wedding coordinator-in-chief.

Gift's parents and siblings, came with a large extended family contingent. Imma spotted Sharon wiping tears. *Tears of joy and sadness? Don't worry Sharon, you're not losing a sister, just gaining a bro.*

In particular, Imma's parents and the siblings who lived in Nigeria and had been forbidden to attend, were all there. At one point Pastor Chima, who learned of Imma's family concerns, turned to his dad.

"Papa, are you happy?"

The sanctuary hushed. Imma's dad took his time rising to his full height. Looking at his wife sitting beside him, at Imma and Gift, and around the room, he bellowed, "Happy as a king!"

The room erupted in resounding applause, and Imma saw relief and tears on many faces. Even his mom was smiling and clapping. Imma finally relaxed, hoping in his heart that Papa had spoken for his entire family, and that everything was going to be all right. Now he was confident that even his siblings overseas would come round. He and Gifty would be accepted and loved by everyone in his family.

Round four won.

Their mouths filled with laughter and their tongues with singing, they each made the ultimate vow: *"I do."*

Round five won. Foretaste of the Prize.

Then the Minister delivered his wedding message and blessing:

The Bible says marriage is a great mystery, but understandable when we recognize that it is an illustration of the way Christ and His church are one. I exhort you therefore to be students of The Word and to grow in your oneness. Then, you will not only solve that mystery, but enjoy it and be ready for the bigger one – the marriage of Jesus in Heaven to His Bride, the church.
True life does not consist in the abundance of material possessions. Together in the institution of marriage, with Jesus as your anchor, the two of you can experience the true and abundant life of righteousness, peace, and joy. He promises to provide all you need, to make you the head and not the tail, and to keep you above and not below – a foretaste of Heaven on earth...

Nodding in agreement and muttering several *Amens*, Imma heaved a huge sigh of relief.

Gift squeezed his hand and smiled.

Not needing the Minister's – or anyone's - permission anymore, Imma planted a lingering, grateful kiss on his wife's lips.

Both knew that Imma had found the answer.

Putting away the marriage certificate in his prized box as they prepared to depart for their honeymoon, his ragged old red diary caught Imma's eye. Flipping it open, he read that entry to Gifty:

December 5, 1979. University of Nigeria, Nsukka.
No one will ever again describe me or my family as deprived. Never again.

Gently drawing Gifty to him, lovingly stroking her beautiful wedding hair, he sat on the bed and read to her the other milestones of his life. She curled her tired body up against him, resting her head on his lap.

"Long day, eh?"

"Long, but unforgettable."

Beaming from ear to ear, he could already hear it now. The high pitched shrieks of children's laughter from little faces that were the perfect blend of Gifty and him. He saw them as they frolicked in the snow. Taking his pen and dreaming of their life and children thriving in America, Imma wrote a new entry in his diary.

THE END

Excerpt of *Deprived no More*, #2 of the *Dream Life* series is included at the back of this boo

NOTES

1. *Thank You*, by Ray Boltz; Album: Thank You (1988); Writer/s: RAYMOND H. BOLTZ; Publisher: Kobalt Music Publishing Ltd., Universal Music Publishing Group.
Lyrics licensed and provided by *LyricFind* (74 out of 324 words from 1 song out of 16 songs in the Album). No copyright on lyrics.
2. *The Tide is High*, The Paragons, 1967; from Album *On the Beach: The Anthology;* Label*: Treasure Isle (UK).* No copyright on lyrics.
3. *Let Your Living Water Flow*. Album - Living Waters, by Jimmy Swaggart; Released: Dec 31, 1984 ℗ 2008 Jim Records. No copyright on lyrics.
4. *The Mesh* – from *The shadows of laughter* by Kwesi Brew, Longman (succeeded by Pearson PLC), 1968 - Poetry - 67 pages (Only 1 page -P. 25 – used out of 67 pages). *Fair Use.*

Dream Life series #2:

DEPRIVED no MORE

Excerpt

For a couple on honeymoon at the start of their dream life together, lots of curious things dominate their minds.

Is 'how are babies made?' supposed to be one of them?

Imma Vine was embarrassed at how such childish curiosity suddenly invaded his thoughts. He blamed his wife Gift's employers, Citizens Bank of Africa, CBA, for interrupting their honeymoon by calling her back to work. The initial pride over how valuable his wife was to her employers as the summons to the office indicated was soon erased by the disappointment that such a big organization wasn't structured to have effective vacation cover. Imma also beat himself up for agreeing to have their honeymoon in a hotel within the city of Lagos where they both worked. *No, it's not my fault. After all my employers, Triumph Merchant Bank, didn't and won't recall me.* It was all CBA's fault!

Because of CBA, there he was alone in the hotel, longing for when his wife would be back from work. And his mind had wandered to the conservative parents' nightmare - when their overly curious kids ask them how babies are made. Remembering what he heard about how such conversation went, he found it good amusement to pass the time.

'Daad, how are babies made?'

'Junior, go ask your mom. She knows everything,' Dad answers. He nudges Junior towards mom in the kitchen, turns back and frantically searches for his car key.

'Mommy, who makes babies?'

'Go ask your dad.'

'I already did and he said it's you that know.'

She marches out to find her husband with junior in tow and just catches the car tail light.

Scooping him in her arms, she answers him.

'Oh, Dad meant to say it's God that knows. He's the one that knows everything, dear. Wait until you can ask Him ok?'

Then she mutters under her breath, 'as for that your dad, I'll kill him today...'

Imma chuckled. He could permit himself such indulgence. *I'm on honeymoon.*

Back home at the end of the one week, Imma looked forward to Gift's announcement that *it* had happened. And then the counting started.

Three weeks. One month. Two months.

No announcement from Gift. And she appeared quite normal. Like before their wedding and honeymoon.

Imma had heard of the various cute ways first time mothers announced such to their husbands:

The casual line dropped with a frown: 'We are expecting.' To which the inattentive husband would respond. 'Who, your mom?'

The swap out his cup for a bottle: Instead of placing a cup by his dinner plate, pour his drink into a baby bottle.

The extra plate on the dinner table: While setting the table, place a kid's plate and cup in addition.

Leave the pregnancy test stick in the bathroom where the husband should see it: Put the hapless guy to an attention to detail test.

The new picture frame in the bedroom: That says, 'I can't wait to meet my daddy.' With wife's hand-written note, 'picture coming soon!'

The piggy bank: That says 'baby fund' on the front. With a note, 'We have nine months to save up.'

Eleven weeks since Honeymoon start, and Imma had not had the pleasure of such pleasant, cute announcement.

Since the cloud of dust that followed Imma's mom's and siblings' rejection of his faith, this was his next major test. He didn't remember discussing with Gift that they wouldn't start a family immediately, and had been praying and believing to receive the fruit of the body pronto. God seemed silent. And Gift too.

Imma wasn't. Only that he just spoke to himself and to God. He restrained from bringing it up with his wife, concerned that he might trigger a negative reaction. *Didn't they say anxiety can make such matters worse?*

Silently, Imma worried. His mind began to play tricks on him, bringing pictures of couples he knew who had not conceived after few years of marriage. On purpose or otherwise.

What would happen to the dream of going to America with their children?

Imma fought off thoughts of never having children of their own just because they hadn't gotten pregnant in over two months since wedding. Don't get ahead of yourself…again!

Then one night he had a dream.

"Imma, if you didn't have a child of your own, would you still worship Me?"

Imma didn't answer immediately. *Trick question!*

"Lord, that would be tough. But why wouldn't You give us a child? Did You not say that if we asked we would receive? That if we delighted in You You would grant us the desire of our heart? Gift and I have met all the conditions and fully expect to…"

Imma stopped when he realized that the Presence was no longer there. He woke up in cold sweat.

As Gift and he drove to work the next morning he still pondered over the dream.

"You are quiet this morning."

"Yeah."

"What's wrong Darling?"

"Nothing… well at least I hope nothing is wrong."

"You're concerned that our babies aren't on the way yet, are you not?"

"How did you know?"

Gifty took and squeezed his free hand as Imma drove with the other.

"I am your wife. One with you. Remember, 'and the two shall be joined together and become one flesh'? You can only hide from me in plain sight…"

"Okay. I will admit that I've been counting the days and they have turned into weeks and months."

"I wondered when you'd bring us to talk about it. I chose to defer to you as the leader of this home to initiate such talk if it was a concern."

Imma squeezed her hand tighter, with genuine remorse written all over his face.

"Appreciate that, Love. Just wasn't sure how you'd handle it."

Gift released his hand, a frown quickly formed.

"Better to find out and we deal with it together in love and faith. We agreed we'd be open with each other on all things. I can't bear you not trusting me to respond in a mature manner."

"I apologize, Love. Forgive me for the communication breakdown. To start on a fresh slate - I had a dream last night."

They just got to Gift's office drop-off at Marina Road, Downtown Lagos Island.

"Got to go. You're forgiven. Let's talk about your dream after work. It better be a good one. Are we having twins?" She laughed for the first time on this traffic-jammed forty five minutes' drive.

Imma found his own laughter too.

Unbuckling her seat belt, she kissed him and alighted from the car.

Suddenly turning back, she leaned in and whispered. "I love you."

"I love you more!" Imma hollered, and sped off to his Awolowo Road Ikoyi office, also on Lagos Island - just fifteen minutes away in light traffic.

Driving home from work, Imma recounted the dream. Gift demonstrated her faith and knowledge of the Bible, confident that just as God repeated His visit to Samson's parents, he would speak to Imma again.

"By the way, what's your stand on adoption?" Gift asked.

"Where's that coming from?"

"Just wondering if that's something we would consider if you're in such a hurry, or…"

"Please stop. Adoption is a great thing, but it's too early." Imma changed the topic to the promotion exercise going on in his office.

That night, Imma had a similar dream. God visited again and picked up the conversation from last night.

"Are you able to give Me a yes or no answer? I can appreciate your rambling of last night, but would like to know clearly."

"Yes, I'll still worship You, Lord. But we know we'll receive our children."

"Good answer. Even if it's by adoption?"

"My wife asked about that this afternoon."

"She is a woman after My Heart. Couples who don't receive their biological children should be happy to receive adopted children. Remember, all you My children were adopted. Jesus Christ is My only Begotten Son, biologically born of Mary by The Holy Spirit."

"You adopted us?"

"Your wife would know that. I am not the Father of every man and woman. You are not guaranteed any special relationship to Me merely by right of creation or your natural birth. It is only by Grace through faith that you are blessed with the opportunity to become My children - by adoption in Christ."

"What a privilege then, to be called Your sons and daughters; to be adopted into Your Family!"

"Another good answer. But you won't have to adopt. I just wanted to know your heart - that You'll love and worship Me regardless. As well, that you'll encourage and appreciate couples who need to adopt; and that you will love adopted children just as I love you all."

Then He announced *it*.

"The due time to conceive your first child has come."

Before Imma could say anything else, The Presence lifted.

Imma jumped up. Coming to, he realized it was another dream. *God has spoken to me!* It lined up with His Word in the Bible that Gifty had referenced. God had visited him - like He visited Samuel's dad, Manoah; John The Baptizer's dad, Zechariah, and Jesus' mom, Mary!

Imma couldn't wait to share the dream with Gifty.

In the third month of their marriage, Gift became pregnant. And in the twelfth month - three days before their wedding anniversary - they welcomed their first child, Jubilee!

Gifty had desired a daughter. Imma was just happy to have a child - girl, boy – but was wise to celebrate in his heart only. *Blessed are they that are open to receive either gender, for they shall not be disappointed.*

The surprise of not having a girl evaporating on day one of his birth, Gifty received their son with exceeding joy and loved him so!

Having gone through another test in the *Dream Life* journey and experienced another rescue, Imma and Gift began to consider whether the *Dream Life* may be more of a process than a destination.

Was it more of who they are already in Christ than what they possess or will have? More of what they will triumph through than a life of zero challenges and deprivation of physical things?

Nevertheless, they were happy that their promise to each other of going to America with their children was alive and well - by faith and patience.

Another sleepless night spent swaying, bouncing and singing to his baby boy, was looming. Michael Card's song, *Wordless Ones*, was Imma's favourite and he launched into the first stanza again.

In Your loving arms we lay This wordless one so new
The incarnation of our love We dedicate to You.

The lack of sleep was nothing compared to the pride and joy that came with being a father. Imma chuckled as he watched Gifty softly snoring, grabbing a couple minutes of sleep for the first time all day.

His little family was growing. So was the *Dream Life* – challenges and all.

Since that first term in university in 1979 Imma had been gripped with IkeChi's 'deprived children' label. As well, he continued to be enamored by Michael Jackson's *Don't Stop 'Till You Get Enough: When does a person become truly non- deprived - When is enough... enough?*
Where does the road to the Dream Life stop? Is there ever a red light, or just green and yellow?

Please see extract from a forthcoming gripping Memoir by Anayo Onwuka

In The Year That Mom Died:
A Memoir

Extract

What is it about mothers?

Isidore Ifezue, my secondary school classmate told me a story of a ghastly accident he witnessed travelling between Onitsha, the commercial nerve-centre of Anambra State and Jos, the capital city of Plateau State – Nigeria.

A car was cutting in front of another at a sharp bend in the road. Unfortunately another vehicle appeared from the opposite and there was no way to maneuver. The multiple collision had the overtaking car driver ejected and under another car that ran over him further down the road - one of the death traps that pass for roads in Nigeria.

Isidore and his fellow passengers got to the scene a few minutes later and courageously jumped out to help. What he remembered most was not the gory picture of that man pinned to the clutches of death. It was the eerie sound of his cry, in between his last gasps of life.

Who will tell my mother?

Who will tell my mother?

It's been forty years since Isidore told me that story. That cry has never left me. My imagination of that gory scene that he painted with his evocative story is as vivid today as it was that day in 1978.

Did that man with only one concern in the world have just his mother? No father, no wife, no kids, no siblings? He probably did.

So, what was special about his mother?

What is it about mothers?

I recall two incidents in my own life when my closeness to and love for my father did not keep my mother's name from being the cry that rose from my very core.

I was a frail eight year old, hunting with my friends for *bush meat* - rats and lizards - in my Umuaro village of Umunumo Town, Nigeria. A civil war had engulfed my country. My ethnic group, the Ibo's, was cleansed, with starvation being the most potent weapon in the 1967-1970 genocide. Meanwhile, most of the world, especially Nigeria's former colonial masters and greatest beneficiary from the mayhem – access to oil - watched.

Even after the war ended in 1970, those of us who did not die from *kwashiorkor*- the extreme malnourishment disease that distended the stomach and made children, female and male, look seven to nine months pregnant - still suffered from unimaginable poverty. The triumphant Nigerian Government ensured that.

So, my friends and I were lucky to be alive and frail. We were happy to not be child soldiers. Just *bush meat* hunters, helping to supplement whatever our parents eked out from subsistence farming and petty trading. I was even luckier than most - my dad was a teacher and got some pay. Some times. But I still needed to do creative things to fill my often half-empty stomach.

And so it was, that on that fateful day, we were pursuing this stubborn rat that was determined to not make it to our kids' firewood grill. But it had met its match - in me. I dived full length to lay hold of it as it raced to disappear into the rabbit hole. The next thing I knew, I was clutching my left knee, gazing at a raw gash. Pure white, it turned red in a split second as blood gushed. I had jumped on a broken bottle. And the rat got away.

My wail of that day as I ran home was the loudest of my young life. My dad and older siblings were home, but all the way only one person made it into my heart-cry.

"*Mama eee*, my leg o!"

"*Mamam eee*, my leg o!"

As my mom ran and met me on the way, she must have thought that I had lost a leg.

A small gash only, but the cry it produced must have begun for me the quest to understand - *what's so pre-eminent about my mother? About a mother?*

The second incident was the day we heard the news of what happened to *De'* Simeon Duru. (In our culture, every male older than you by more than a few years is "De'", short for *Dede* - "Uncle". And such senior female is "Da'", short for *Dada*, loosely interpreted, "Auntie").

A successful civil servant earlier at Enugu, the then capital of our East Central State, he had gotten a scholarship to study in Scotland. He returned home for the first time in the one year since leaving his two young kids and a wife pregnant with the third. During that vacation, he travelled with another kinsman to visit his age-mate, friend and the most prominent son of our village, Professor Ethelbert Nwakuche Chukwu - who had been recently appointed Vice Chancellor of the Federal University of Technology, Yola, Adamawa State in the North East.

His co-traveler, De' Lawrence Uche, came back without him and with a tale that we wish till today he didn't tell.

For a leg-stretch and bathroom break in the long, over fourteen hours journey on the interesting highway, their Bus had stopped by a bridge. Most of the passengers went to the nearby river to freshen themselves. De' Simeon slipped and the fast-flowing river swept him away. Hours of frantic search by the mobilized native fishermen had yielded no results and they dispelled any hope that he was alive. As at the time *De'* Lawrence was persuaded to leave the scene and continue home to inform our people, our beloved De' Simeon's body had not been recovered.

'Simeon is dead!' Lawrence moaned.

I happened to be at his home when he got there and shared that news. A wailing arose. All I remember was taking off, running and screaming.

"*Mama eee! Mamam eee*! *De'* Simeon! *De'* Simeon...!"

My mom left my dad and all others in our home, running out to me.

"What? What about Simeon?" she shouted, already joining the dirge. She knew her son. When I ran to her like that, it was not good.

What is it about my mother? About mothers?

My mother. She brought me into the world, loved me and nurtured me. Her really tough love discipline - so that I would not grow up lazy and irresponsible - was totally legal in her eyes.

And then she died.

Leaving behind many of her children. Including me.

Deprived of a mother, I was left to flail in the vast ocean, my dream life now resembling my worst nightmare.

That voice that hasn't gone away since childhood: *Eat your vegetables. Pick up your toys...! Say your prayer before you sleep. Have you brushed your teeth? Make your bed*!

Whose voice is it? That I really heard and still hear?

Papa was the "faith" parent. He believed I would do what I needed to do. If I liked. Or maybe he knew I would "hear" from Mama. *Good cop, bad cop.*

Savouring my independence as an adult pursuing the dream, things still ring in my ear from nowhere. Work before pleasure. Earn your play. Sit before you recline.

Who's clanging those bells?

Who told those folklore and proverbs?
*Ebele ako (*male sheep - ram*) asked its child: how many times will same thing happen to you before you learn the lesson?*
The stubborn fly will follow the corpse to its grave.

She left me and died. But the voice continues to resound; and the bells and teaching moments keep ringing.

I still have to grapple with wanting to pick up the phone on a Saturday morning and remembering that Mama will not be at the other end of the line to answer me. My immediate older brother Chidiya, who lives in Pueblo North Carolina USA, laughed at me when I sobbed pouring out my frustration to him over the phone.

"Please call her. If she answers you, let me know so I can call her too," he said, laughing and making jest of it. I managed to chuckle through my tears. But my Saturday *Mama Calls* desire still feels entitled.

I'm not making any plans to go home anytime soon. When Papa left me, us, and died, Mama was there, ensuring that the home where we were raised was not empty. Not anymore.

Pursuing the Dream Life, sharing progress or disappointment with Mama made it feel better. Even when she disagreed, the challenge of convincing her and the joy of seeing her respect my decision or acknowledge the good results, gave life to the pursuit.

Now that she has left me and died, I am left to grow up all on my own. Well, not exactly - just without my mother and having to look elsewhere for the drive she physically provided. That's what motherless babies, children, men and women have to do.

Who will be my mother now?

Who will adopt this fatherless, motherless child – this *poor* orphan?

Made in the USA
Middletown, DE
28 November 2018